HOWDY!

Welcome to the Circle C. My name is Andi Carter. If you are a new reader, here's a quick roundup of my family, friends, and adventures:

I'm a tomboy who lives on a huge cattle ranch near Fresno, California, in the exciting 1880s. I would rather ride my palomino mare, Taffy, than do anything else. I mean well, but trouble just seems to follow me around.

Our family includes my mother, Elizabeth, my ladylike older sister, Melinda, and my three older brothers: Justin (a lawyer), Chad, and Mitch. I love them, but sometimes they treat me like a pest. My father was killed in a ranch accident a few years ago.

In **Long Ride Home**, Taffy is stolen and it's my fault. I set out to find my horse and end up far from home and in a heap of trouble.

In **Dangerous Decision**, I nearly trample my new teacher in a horse race with my friend Cory. Later, I have to make a life-or-death choice.

Next, I discover I'm the only one who doesn't know the Carter **Family Secret**, and it turns my world upside down.

In **San Francisco Smugglers**, a flood sends me to school in the city for two months. My new roommate, Jenny, and I discover that the little Chinese servant-girl in our school is really a slave.

Trouble with Treasure is what Jenny, Cory, and I find when we head into the mountains with Mitch to pan for gold.

And then I may lose my beloved horse, Taffy, if I tell what I saw in **Price of Truth**.

Now saddle up and ride into my latest adventure!

Andi

ANDREA CARTER AND THE

Family Secret

CIRCLE C BEGINNINGS

Andi's Pony Trouble
Andi's Indian Summer
Andi's Fair Surprise
Andi's Scary School Days
Andi's Lonely Little Foal
Andi's Circle C Christmas

CIRCLE C STEPPING STONES

Andi Saddles Up
Andi Under the Big Top
Andi Lassos Trouble
Andi to the Rescue
Andi Dreams of Gold
Andi Far from Home

CIRCLE C ADVENTURES

Andrea Carter and the Long Ride Home
Andrea Carter and the Dangerous Decision
Andrea Carter and the Family Secret
Andrea Carter and the San Francisco Smugglers
Andrea Carter and the Trouble with Treasure
Andrea Carter and the Price of Truth

CIRCLE C MILESTONES

Thick as Thieves: An Andrea Carter Book
Heartbreak Trail: An Andrea Carter Book
The Last Ride: An Andrea Carter Book
Courageous Love: An Andrea Carter Book

ANNIVERSARY EDITION • 3

ANDREA CARTER AND THE

Family Secret

SUSAN K. MARLOW

Kregel
Publications

Andrea Carter and the Family Secret
© 2008, 2018 by Susan K. Marlow

Published by Kregel Publications, a division of Kregel, Inc., 2450 Oak Industrial Dr. NE, Grand Rapids, MI 49505.

Scripture quotations are from the King James Version.

ISBN 978-0-8254-4502-6

Printed in the United States of America
18 19 20 21 22 23 24 25 26 27 / 5 4 3 2 1

CONTENTS

1. Unexpected Encounter .9
2. Cory Speaks His Mind 18
3. Worse Than Aunt Rebecca 24
4. Betrayed 30
5. Journey into the Past. 37
6. Homecoming 47
7. Return to the Creek .56
8. A Handful of Nieces .62
9. Trouble in the Schoolyard 71
10. More Trouble 77
11. An Empty House 85
12. A Visit from TJ 92
13. An Afternoon Ride .97
14. A Dangerous Discovery. 103
15. The Storm 112
16. A Chilly Welcome. .118
17. Into the Night. 126
18. No Place to Run 133
19. Farewell. 140

Chapter One

UNEXPECTED ENCOUNTER

SAN JOAQUIN VALLEY, CALIFORNIA, FALL 1880

When twelve-year-old Andrea Carter brought her palomino mare to a stop next to her favorite fishing spot, she expected to find a creek full of trout.

Instead, she found a dead man.

He lay sprawled facedown in the middle of the creek bed. Thick, dark mud plastered his clothes and head. One hand dangled limply in a pool of dirty water. The creek, which Andi was sure would be filled after two rare downpours this week, trickled past the lifeless stranger in shallow, muddy channels.

Andi swallowed her shock and fought to calm her racing heart. She knew she should dismount and see if the man was really dead, but her feet stayed frozen in the stirrups.

Gripping Taffy's reins, Andi glanced behind her shoulder at the two riders galloping toward her. *This is what I get for always coming in first. Next time we race, Cory can win. Let him find the surprises.*

"I'm not going near any dead man. Uh-uh. Not by myself." Her voice shook. "You hear me, Taffy? We stay put until Cory and Rosa catch up."

A moment later, Cory reined his chestnut gelding alongside Andi. "You beat me, but it wasn't a fair race. I didn't see that little gully until . . ." His voice trailed off. "What's wrong, Andi?"

She pointed toward the creek bed. "Him."

Cory's mouth dropped open. "What in the world?"

Rosa pulled up on her horse. When she saw the body, she gasped.

"*¿Quién es? ¿Qué pasó?*" She crossed herself and mumbled a quick prayer.

Andi shook her head. "I don't know who he is, and I don't know what happened. I didn't want to do anything until you two got here."

"We're here now. Let's go see." Cory dismounted and tossed his reins around a scraggly branch of an oak tree. "Maybe he's not as dead as he looks. We should at least get him out of the mud."

"I reckon you're right," Andi said, but she made no move to leave her saddle.

Cory chuckled. "It's a good thing the creek isn't as full as you promised, or he'd have drowned for sure—I mean, if he isn't dead already." He squinted up at Andi. "Come on."

Andi slid off Taffy and dropped the reins to ground-tie her horse. She didn't find anything funny about a dead man half-buried in the creek bottom. She looked up at Rosa, still astride her mount. "Aren't you coming?"

Rosa shook her head. "I will stay with the horses."

For once, Andi agreed with her cautious Mexican friend. This wasn't the kind of scrape Andi usually stumbled into. Knocking down the schoolmaster during a spur-of-the-moment horse race or breaking a window playing baseball was more her style; or maybe a close call with an unbroken horse; or barging into her brother's law office during an important meeting with a client.

But not this. Not finding a *dead* man.

She shivered, in spite of the blistering California heat.

"Andi! You coming?" Cory hollered and clambered down the steep creek bank. "Hurry."

Andi sighed. "I better help him," she told Rosa, and scurried after her friend.

She grimaced all the way down the embankment. Each step sank her deeper into the muck. By the time she reached Cory's side, her overalls were splattered with mud. She bent over the man and drew a sharp breath. Up close he looked *very* dead. His face was ashen between the streaks of dirt.

"Is he"—she swallowed—"is he dead?"

Cory shook his head. "Nope. I shook him, and he moaned."

Andi let out her breath. "That's good."

"But he's in bad shape," Cory said. "There's no telling how long he's been here. We need to get him out of the sun and into some shade." He reached under the man's shoulders and yanked. Nothing happened. "He's stuck."

Andi jumped up to help, but no amount of grunting and groaning and heaving moved the man so much as an inch. She let the man's arms drop to the ground. "What're we going to do? Even with Rosa's help, we'll never get him out on our own. We're not strong enough."

"One of us could ride to your place and bring back some of the ranch hands to help," Cory suggested.

"That would take too long." Andi glanced up. Rosa had dismounted and was sitting in the shade of an oak. "I've got an idea. I'll be right back." She squished her way up the embankment and hurried to Taffy.

"Is the *hombre* dead?" Rosa asked.

"Not yet." Andi grabbed a coil of rope from her saddle horn and ran back to Cory. She thrust it into his hands. "Here. Put his arms and shoulders through the loop. Then cinch it up."

Cory went to work.

Andi put two fingers to her mouth and whistled. Reins dangling, Taffy stepped to the edge of the creek bank.

"Rosa!" Andi called. When her friend appeared, Andi tossed the rest of the rope up the incline. "Tie it around the saddle horn. Then slowly back Taffy up when we say so."

Rosa caught the rope and nodded.

"I'm ready," Cory said from his place next to the unconscious man. "I hope this doesn't kill him."

Andi signaled to Rosa, who began to lead the palomino away from the creek.

Andi and Cory placed their hands on the man's limp form to steady him. The rope went taut, and the man moaned. Then with a loud sucking sound, the mud gave way and he slid quickly toward the bank.

"Hold up!" Cory shouted. The rope went slack. "Now pull him along real careful, Rosa." Slipping and sliding, they guided the stranger up and over the creek bank and into the shade.

"I don't think that did him any good." Andi crouched beside the body. "He looks terrible. Do you reckon he's still alive?"

Cory dropped down beside her. "Let's roll him over and see."

As soon as they turned him over, Andi shook him. "Mister, are you all right? Wake up." She waited for a reply, but none came. The stranger lay still as death.

"Go get your canteen," she told Cory. "A little water might do the trick. I caught Mitch napping under a tree last Sunday and poured a pitcher of water over his head. I never saw anybody wake up so fast."

"Bet he was hoppin' mad," Cory said. He sprang to his feet and retrieved the canteen. "Did he get after you for soaking him?"

"Yep. I ran, but not fast enough. Mitch caught me and tossed me in the horse trough." She grinned. "It was so hot that I didn't mind. We both ended up having a good laugh." She unscrewed the canteen lid. "Here goes."

A stream of lukewarm water spilled onto the man's face.

It was a miracle the way the man yelped and tried to sit up. He slapped his hands against his face and sputtered, "You tryin' to drown me?" Then he gasped and collapsed with a groan.

Andi's fear faded. "It worked. Even on a half-dead fella." She sat back on her heels, pleased. "Thank you, God," she whispered.

"That's for sure," Cory agreed. He brought his face close to the stranger's. "You know how close you came to never waking up? We pulled you out of the creek, and none too soon. Another day or two in this heat and you'd have been buzzard bait."

"*Cory!*"

"He's right." The stranger rubbed his face, took a deep breath, and sat up. "Reckon I owe you kids some thanks." He studied Andi through bloodshot eyes and pointed at the canteen. "Mind if I put some of that on the inside?"

She handed it over.

The man bent his head back and took gulp after gulp of water before emptying the rest of it over his head. He tossed the canteen aside and ran his fingers through his dripping hair. "Much obliged." He scooted back until he was leaning against the tree trunk. His hands shook. "I feel like a herd of cattle ran right over the top of me."

"Who are you?" Andi asked. "And how did you end up in the middle of the creek?"

The stranger closed his eyes and let out a long, deep breath. "Name's TJ Silver. I have no idea how I got here. I don't even know where I am." He opened his eyes. "This California?"

"Yes."

Mr. Silver nodded. "Good. Last thing I remember was finishing up a very unfriendly game of cards with the worst poker players I ever laid eyes on." He settled himself more comfortably against the tree. "I cleaned 'em out pretty good, but I guess they were sore losers and wanted their money back. I don't recall exactly how they did it, but I think they got it back."

He winced and clutched his stomach with both arms. "Something doesn't feel right."

Andi and Cory carefully pushed the man's arms aside. A bright red streak showed through his muddy shirt. Cory tugged open the fabric and gave a low whistle. "Boy, oh boy, mister. Looks like somebody sliced you up good. All your moving around must've broke it open."

Mr. Silver dropped his gaze to his stomach. "Don't remember how that happened."

"How long has it been since that card game?" Andi stared at the gash. It was seeping blood slowly but steadily.

"Wednesday night."

"Today's Saturday." Andi frowned. "With a wound like that it's no wonder you passed out. You should see a doctor. Fresno's not far, not more than a couple of hours."

Cory handed TJ the bandana from around his neck.

"I don't need a doctor." Mr. Silver took the kerchief with a curt nod of thanks. "I've lasted this long. I'll go on living."

"Are you sure?" Andi asked.

"Yeah." He stuffed the fabric inside his shirt and pressed his hand against his belly. "I just need a few days of rest and some grub, and I'll be on my way." He closed his eyes and leaned back. "If you'll hobble my gelding, I'd appreciate it."

Andi frowned. "We didn't see any horse."

"He's around here somewhere. Could you do a fella a favor and see if you can find him, Miss . . . ?" He paused and gave her a weak smile.

"Carter," Andi responded. "Andi Carter." She nodded to her friends. "This is Cory Blake and Rosa Garduño."

"A pleasure," came the man's reply. "Now . . . about my horse?"

It didn't take long to find the gelding. He was grazing on the parched, brown grass not too far from where his rider had ended up in the creek. The horse lifted his head and gave a challenging whinny when the three young riders drew near.

Andi brought Taffy to a stop and dismounted.

"He doesn't look friendly," Cory warned. "Don't get too close. Just grab the reins and lead him back."

Andi yanked open her saddlebags. With a confident smile she brought out an apple and waved it at Cory. "I don't know any horse who'd turn down a treat like this." She approached the large bay gelding with cautious steps. "Easy, fella. Look what I've got for you."

The horse pricked up his ears but kept his distance.

"I'm not going to hurt you," Andi said. "Come here."

The gelding shook his mane, snorted, and took a few steps toward Andi. His neck and chest were covered with old, dried sweat.

"Be careful, Andi. Don't spook him."

Andi threw Cory a disgusted look. "Be quiet." She moved closer. "It's all right, fella. Come get the apple, and I'll take you to your rider. Then I'll get rid of that nasty saddle. What do you say?"

Ears pricked forward, the horse walked over and took a greedy bite. By the time he chomped the rest of the apple, Andi had snagged the reins. "I've got him. Let's go."

Cory shook his head. "One of these days you're gonna meet a horse that doesn't like you. Then what'll you do?"

"I haven't met one yet I couldn't sweet-talk into behaving." She gave the bay a friendly pat and mounted Taffy.

"Oh, no?" Cory teased. "What about that wild stallion of Chad's? I seem to remember hearing about a ruckus out at your place last spring. Let's see . . ." He snapped his fingers. "That's it! You didn't get along real well with that big black horse and you almost—"

"I don't want to talk about that." Andi scowled at him.

Cory chuckled. "I'm sure you don't."

Back at the oak, Andi loosened the cinch on the stranger's horse, and the heavy saddle tumbled to the ground. Freed at last from his burden, the horse lay down and rolled.

Andi grinned. "That feels a lot better, doesn't it?"

"You really gonna stay here," Cory was saying to the injured man, "when you're so bad off?"

Mr. Silver's lips twisted into a crooked smile. "I don't feel like bouncing around on a horse for a couple hours just to see a doc. I'm feeling much improved already."

He turned to Andi, who was at work hobbling the gelding. "Could

I stay up here on your ranch, Miss Carter? If you want to play Good Samaritan, you could rustle up some grub and bring it out here the next few days. It sure would help me out."

Andi traded glances with her friends. It was her decision. After all, it was *her* family's ranch this poor fellow had collapsed on. Cory lived in town, too far away to run errands back and forth. Rosa would go along with whatever Andi decided, even if she didn't approve.

By the look she was giving Andi, Rosa clearly did *not* approve. "You should do nothing until you let your brothers know about this stranger," she said in rapid Spanish. "*Señor* Chad will decide what is best to do."

"Chad's too busy haying to be bothered. Besides, it's only for a few days," Andi replied, her Spanish just as fluent as her friend's. "The least we can do is bring him a few supplies."

"I don't mean to cause an argument between you and your friends," Mr. Silver said. "All I'm asking for is a little something to hold me over. You can ride by on a fast horse and toss it to me if you're uneasy. I'll be off your ranch before you know it."

He ducked his head. "I'd be much obliged if you didn't mention my being up here, though. The rowdies who came after me the other night might still be hanging around the area, and eager to finish what they started."

Poor Mr. Silver would be a sitting duck if word got around of a wounded stranger up in the high pasture. "Oh, I wouldn't think of it," Andi promised. "You can stay. I've got lunch in my saddlebags." She jumped up.

A grateful smile cracked Mr. Silver's dirt-streaked face. "That's right neighborly of you," he called after her. "Thanks."

Andi brought the contents of her saddlebags and laid everything out under the tree—two roast beef sandwiches and half a dozen molasses cookies. "Sorry, but your horse ate my apple."

Cory and Rosa exchanged a glance, and soon their lunches joined Andi's.

Mr. Silver eyed the food with a hungry gleam and reached for a sandwich. "This'll hold me. You three have done me a good turn. I won't be forgetting it." He bit into the sandwich.

"I'm glad we could help, Mr. Silver," Andi said. "I hope you heal up real fast."

"My friends call me TJ," he said between mouthfuls.

Andi grabbed Taffy's reins and swung up into the saddle. "All right, TJ. Take care of yourself. I don't know when I can bring you more food, but I'll try."

"Can't ask for more than that." TJ waved. "Thanks again."

Cory and Rosa joined Andi, and the three riders headed out.

Chapter Two

CORY SPEAKS HIS MIND

Her friends' silent, disapproving looks bored into Andi during the ride back to the ranch house. It was clear they didn't think she should keep quiet about TJ staying on the Circle C. A sliver of worry that maybe she wasn't doing the right thing pricked Andi's conscience, but she shrugged it off.

They're just a couple of fraidy-cats, worried about nothing. What's wrong with being kind to a poor drifter? He sure seems grateful.

Cory shook his head, as if he could read her thoughts. "You're making a mistake," he finally said. Then he touched his heels to his chestnut's flank and galloped away.

Andi nudged Taffy and went after Cory. "Hold on," she demanded when she'd caught up. Both horses slowed to a walk. "Go ahead and spill what you want to say before you burst."

"All right, I will." Cory shifted in his saddle. "There's something not quite right. TJ's friendly—no doubt about it—and he seems grateful we fished him out of the creek, but"—he nodded at Rosa, who had trotted up alongside Andi—"Rosa's right. You should tell your brothers he's up in your high pasture."

"During the middle of our final alfalfa harvest?" Andi shook her head. "Chad would not be happy. I'll tell him about it later. By that time, TJ will be long gone." She rolled her eyes. "You were sure eager to help him when he looked half dead. Now you're acting scared. Why?"

"I'm *not* scared!" Cory snorted. "I've just got questions."

"What kind of questions?"

Cory pulled his horse to a stop and narrowed his eyes. "Well, tell me this. How did that fella know this was *your* ranch?"

The question drew Andi up short. She stared at Cory and tried to remember what she'd said to TJ. She'd told him her name and the names of her friends. Had she come right out and said he was on the Circle C? No. It hadn't come up. So how—

"He wasn't even sure he was in California until we told him," Cory said. "Yet he asked if he could stay on your ranch a few days. Not my ranch. *Your* ranch. For all anybody can see, this could be open range." He gave Andi a triumphant look. "Explain *that!*"

Andi couldn't explain it. "I must have mentioned the ranch."

"You didn't," Cory said. "TJ Silver's hiding something. And the fact that he knows this is your spread isn't the only thing, I bet."

"So what? It's a free country. As long as he doesn't bother anybody, he can hide what he likes. I'm just getting him supplies to help him on his way."

"What if he's an outlaw? Maybe he holds up stagecoaches. Or robs banks."

"That's a crazy notion."

Cory's look turned stubborn. "No, it's not."

Andi sighed. "Why can't TJ Silver be what he appears to be—a poor drifter down on his luck and in need of a helping hand? The Bible says we're supposed to help strangers in need, because we might be entertaining angels unawares."

"TJ Silver's no angel," Cory insisted. "I'm glad we saved his life, but that doesn't mean I can't be suspicious."

Andi grew silent. If Cory got it into his head that TJ was a threat, there was no telling what he would do. He might even tell Chad.

Andi preferred to stay out of her brother's way during the busy days of haying and harvesting. He was grumpy, and finding out a stranger was squatting on Circle C land would only make him grumpier.

Besides, Andi felt good knowing she'd brought a man back from the brink of death. She wanted to go on helping him get better.

It's time to change the subject and get Cory's mind on something else.

Andi knew exactly what to say. "Hey, Cory. Why don't you stop by the house and get something to eat before you head home? You gave your lunch to TJ, and it's a long, hot ride back to town."

Cory brightened at the mention of food. "That's not a bad idea. Thanks."

Andi grinned at her success in distracting her friend and urged Taffy into an easy lope. She cut through the recently harvested hay fields and leaped over one of the new irrigation ditches that carried water from the San Joaquin River to the thirsty acres of alfalfa, orchards, and vineyards.

Cory and Rosa hurried to catch up. A few minutes later, they pulled their horses to a dusty standstill in the middle of the yard.

Andi slid from Taffy's back and flung the reins over the hitching rail. She glanced around the yard. A number of cowhands were guiding a wagonload of alfalfa up against the hay barn. The sounds of creaking wheels, jingling harnesses, and sharp commands to the horses filled the air.

"Hey, what're you doing back so soon?" Sid McCoy, the Carters' longtime foreman, strolled over and tweaked one of Andi's braids. "I thought we got rid of you for the afternoon."

"The creek's just a trickle," Andi said. "No fishing today." She shot Cory a warning look.

Sid pushed back his wide-brimmed hat and looked at Cory. "Ever think about hiring on as water boy next summer? It's too much for Rosa's brother to handle alone. I could use another fine, strapping lad like yourself."

"Pa'd skin the hide offa me if I took a ranch job," Cory said. "He needs my help running the livery. You know that, Mr. McCoy."

Sid shrugged. "It don't hurt to ask now and again."

"I'll work for you, Sid," Andi piped up. "I know everything about cattle, and I can lasso better than—"

"If I've told you once, Miss Andi, I've told you a hundred times. Those jobs ain't fittin' for a young lady. No use begging. You'll have to content yourself with other ways to earn your keep."

Andi scuffed the dust with her boot. "It don't hurt to ask now and again." She mimicked the tone the foreman had used with Cory.

Sid's wrinkled, weather-beaten face cracked a smile. He waggled a finger at Andi. "Enough of your sass, miss. Go on with you now, and stay out of my way. We still got tons of hay to put up today, and I don't want to see any of those loads landing on you or your friends. *¿Comprende?*"

Andi nodded.

Sid pointed to the hitching rail. "Don't forget about those horses, either. It's mighty hot." He removed his hat and wiped a dirty sleeve across his forehead. Then he slammed his hat on his head, gave Andi a farewell nod, and headed back to the hay wagon.

Andi turned away from the hay loading and glanced at her family's two-story house. With its white stucco walls and red-tiled roof, it sparkled like a cool oasis in the middle of the desert. It appeared the perfect place to rest and relax this afternoon, but she knew that those thick, inviting walls hid a beehive of activity.

A nudge from Cory brought her around. "So, are we going to get something to eat or not?"

Andi grinned. "Let's head for the cookhouse and see what Cook's fixing for the hands. I don't want to show up at the house just yet. If Mother sees me back so soon, she'll put me to work squishing apples or some other horribly dull job."

"And *mi mamá* too," Rosa said, clearly enjoying her free hours. "There is always much to do in the big house."

"We can eat with the hands?" Cory smacked his lips.

"Sure!" Andi turned her back on the house and took off across the yard. As she passed the carriage house, her steps slowed, then stopped. Tied up in front of the building stood a buckskin horse hitched to a shiny black buggy. "Somebody's here."

Cory and Rosa stopped beside her. Cory shrugged. "So?" He plucked her sleeve. "Come on. Let's eat."

Andi brushed his hand away and circled the buggy, scowling. "Nobody told me we were having company today." She shot a troubled glance toward the house, then back at the buggy.

Cory rolled his eyes. "So what? A neighbor came by to talk to your brothers."

"When neighbors talk to my brothers they come by on horseback, not in a hired rig. Take a closer look. It's one of your pa's rigs."

Cory came alongside Andi and swiped a finger over the lettering of Blake's Livery. "You're right. But I still don't see why you care. Aren't you hungry?"

Andi bit her lip. "You don't understand. The only person who ever comes calling without warning is Aunt Rebecca. She's famous for her surprise visits. And every time she comes, she tries to talk Mother into sending me to the city for a month or two. She wants to turn me into a young lady and send me to some highfalutin girls' school."

Cory chuckled.

"It's not funny. One of these days Mother's going to give in. You can only say no to Aunt Rebecca so many times." She made a face.

"Oh, Andi! Lots of folks hire rigs, not just your rich San Francisco aunt. It could be anyone. Why don't you go up to the house and see?"

The sudden bang of a door slamming saved Andi from having to reply to Cory's sensible suggestion. She shaded her eyes and looked across the yard. Her twenty-seven-year-old brother was striding purposefully toward the barn.

"Chad!" she hollered. It would be best to find out what Aunt Rebecca wanted beforehand, rather than stumble into the house unprepared.

Chad turned. He gave Rosa and Cory a friendly wave and hurried over to Andi. "I'm glad you're back. Saves me the trouble of fetching you home, especially when I've got too much else to do." He jerked his thumb toward the house. "You'd best go inside. Mother wants to talk to you."

Andi froze. "Is it Aunt Rebecca? Has she come to drag me back to San Francisco with her?"

Chad's face was pale under his dark tan. "No, little sister. It's not Aunt Rebecca. It's worse."

Chapter Three

WORSE THAN AUNT REBECCA

Andi grabbed Chad's arm. Chills raced up her spine. How could anything be worse than a visit from Aunt Rebecca? "What do you mean *worse*? If it's not Aunt Rebecca, who's here?"

"Hey, Andi." Cory glanced uneasily at Chad. "I'm going to pass on your offer to eat with the hands. Thanks, but I better get home." Without waiting for a reply, he scurried back to his horse. Rosa trailed behind, untied her horse, and disappeared into the barn without so much as a good-bye.

Andi dug her fingers into Chad's arm and shook it. "Why does Mother want to see me?" She tried to think of a reason, and what it might have to do with a hired rig from town. What if—

Oh no! She flushed. "It's not Mrs. Evans, is it? Come to complain about her missing flowers? Whatever she said I did, it's not true. I haven't gone anywhere near her yard since—" She broke off at the faraway look in her brother's blue eyes. He wasn't even listening.

"Chad?" She shook him, harder this time. "Tell me what's going on. Am I in trouble?"

Chad blinked and seemed to come to himself. "No. It's nothing like that." He laid a gentle hand on her shoulder and squeezed. "It's not my place to tell you. If you go in the house, Mother will explain everything." He smiled. "I'm sorry I gave you a start. I'm . . . I'm sorry about everything." He turned and walked away.

Andi watched Chad's departure with bewilderment. Whatever was disturbing him lay just inside the walls of the house. Whenever somebody as cocksure of himself as Chad started apologizing for no apparent reason, it meant something was terribly wrong.

She took a deep breath, squared her shoulders, and headed around back to the kitchen door. *At least it's not Aunt Rebecca,* she told herself, relieved. *That's something. What can possibly be worse than a visit from Aunt Rebecca?*

Pushing through the back door, Andi entered the kitchen. The sharp, sweet smell of simmering apples greeted her. "Mother?"

Her mother was nowhere in sight. Neither was Luisa, their housekeeper, nor Nila, the cook. Across the room, a huge kettle of apples sat on the cookstove, pushed away from the fire. Dozens of empty canning jars were lined up on the oak table in the middle of the kitchen. A canister of sugar lay open. It was clear something had interrupted a day of putting up applesauce.

The door leading to the dining room burst open and Andi's older sister Melinda hurried in. She was carrying a tiny girl with round, blue eyes and a head full of tangled, golden curls. When the child saw Andi, she popped a dirty thumb in her mouth and buried her face in Melinda's blouse.

"Look, Andi," Melinda said. "Isn't she the sweetest thing you ever saw? Her name's Hannah." She brushed by Andi and set Hannah in a chair. Then she crossed the kitchen, opened the icebox, and pulled out a pitcher of milk.

Andi didn't move.

Hannah reached out her grubby hands and whined.

"Just a minute, sweetie." Melinda filled a glass with milk and carefully placed it in the child's outstretched hands.

Andi watched in astonishment while her older sister hovered over the bedraggled little girl. She had planned to ask the first person she saw what was going on, but at the sight of Hannah, she could only point and stammer, "W-who's that?"

"I told you. Her name's Hannah." Melinda paused and looked Andi over. "You look like you've been stomping around in a muddy creek. Have you?"

"Not exactly. I—"

"You'd better change your clothes before you meet Katherine," Melinda ordered. "I don't want her to see you looking like a grubby ranch hand. Why can't you ever . . . ?" Her voice trailed off in a weary sigh. "Oh, never mind. Just go upstairs and put on a dress."

Andi stared at her sister. Melinda wasn't usually so bossy. Something must have really gotten her worked up, and Andi didn't have to look far to find the reason—the mysterious Katherine. "Who's Katherine?"

Melinda's cheeks reddened. She now seemed at a loss for words. "She's . . . she's . . . uh . . ." She hugged Hannah and blurted, "She's Hannah's mother."

"That doesn't tell me anything," Andi snapped. "Why is she here?"

"Change your clothes and go into the parlor. Mother will explain." She turned her attention away from Andi and steadied Hannah's glass so she could finish the last few drops of milk.

"First Chad. Now you." Andi jammed her hands on her hips. "Mother will explain *what*?"

When her sister didn't answer, Andi turned on her heel and headed for the dining room door.

Melinda leaped up and blocked Andi's way. "You can't go in there looking like that. Use the back stairs and get cleaned up." Her expression softened. "Please." Her blue eyes pleaded for Andi's cooperation.

With a shrug, Andi gave in. "All right, Melinda. If it means that much to you, I'll clean up before I meet this Katherine person. Whoever she is, she's sure got you in a dither."

Andi ducked into the narrow back staircase that led from the kitchen to the second floor. She took the steps two at a time and nearly collided with her brother Mitch, who was passing through the hallway at the top of the stairs.

Mitch caught Andi up and spun her around. "What do you think, Sis? Isn't it grand?" He set her down. Then he ran his fingers through his sandy hair and shook his head. "I still can't believe it. It's a miracle."

Andi backed away from Mitch, tongue-tied. Had everyone gone *loco*? Chad was strangely quiet, Melinda was bossy, and Mitch? Well, Mitch was behaving like a giddy schoolboy on the last day of school.

Before Andi could ask Mitch why he was hanging around the house instead of putting up hay, he started down the wide, main steps to the foyer. He ran his hand lightly along the polished banister and began whistling a lively tune.

Andi caught her breath. For one horrible second, she thought her brother might leap onto the banister railing and slide the rest of the way. She exhaled in relief when he slowed his descent to a walk and reached the bottom of the stairs.

What is the matter with everybody? Andi wondered. She entered her room and peeled off her muddy overalls and wrinkled shirt. She tossed them beside the door and threw open her wardrobe. *A dress. On a Saturday afternoon. To meet a stranger everybody's all fired up about.*

Andi wished she'd stayed at the creek. But no, that would not have lasted. Somebody—probably Chad—would have fetched her home. She could imagine Chad's reaction at seeing TJ, when he expected to find only Andi and her friends.

Andi sighed. Her Saturday afternoon was quickly dissolving into a muddle. *Oh, I wish I knew who this Katherine person is!*

Her thoughts tumbled one on top of the other as she pulled a simple, calico-sprigged cotton dress over her head and struggled to button it up. Her fingers fumbled at the task, and she wondered— not for the first time—whose silly idea it was to design a dress with buttons down the back. With a defiant tug, she tied the wide blue sash, hurried to her vanity, and glanced in the mirror.

Uh-oh. Her face was sunburned and dotted with splatters of dried mud. For the first time since leaving the creek, she looked at her hands. Not only were they dirty but they were also smeared with streaks of dried blood—TJ Silver's blood. Andi suddenly felt grateful for Melinda's insistence that she clean up.

She scrubbed her hands and face until the water in the porcelain bowl turned black. Then she quickly plaited her hair into two fresh braids, took a deep breath, and decided it was time to find out what was going on. With her heart in her throat, she headed for the stairs.

When Andi reached the parlor, she stopped just shy of the doorway. A soft murmur of voices came from the room, but she couldn't make out what they were saying. The door stood open, so Andi could easily enter.

But she didn't. She stood on the threshold and waited for Mother to invite her in. While she waited, she took the opportunity to observe the young woman sitting on the settee.

She's pretty—or she would be if she smiled, Andi thought.

The woman had wide blue eyes, a pert little nose, and a strong chin that suggested she knew how to take care of herself. Her thick, dark curls were pulled back into a tired-looking chignon off her neck. A few rebellious strands of hair had escaped and lay curling around her face. She clasped and unclasped her hands in her lap and adjusted the folds of her tattered skirt.

Then, to Andi's astonishment, Mother reached out and took the woman's trembling hands. She brought them to her lips and brushed a tender kiss over them. The woman's shoulders shook, and she began to sob in earnest.

Andi dropped her gaze and stepped back. She knew better than to spy on her mother and a person in obvious distress. It was time either to make herself known or to slip away.

"Mother?"

Both women glanced up.

"You wanted to see me?"

"Indeed I do." Mother rose and greeted Andi with a smile that lit up her whole face. "Come in." She wrapped her arm around Andi's waist and drew her into the parlor. "Let's sit down, shall we?" She turned to the young woman. "Katherine, this is Andrea."

Andi slowly found her seat. She couldn't pull her gaze from the stranger sitting across from her. Up close, she was even more striking.

Katherine gave Andi a tiny smile. "Hello, Andrea. It's been a very, *very* long time since I saw you last."

Andi looked at her mother for an explanation.

"Sweetheart," Mother said in a shaky voice, "this is Katherine . . . your sister."

Chapter Four

BETRAYED

Andi reeled at her mother's words. She leaped from the settee and gaped at the stranger. "My *what?*"

Her *sister?* Impossible. She couldn't have lived her entire life without knowing she had another sister. The idea was ridiculous. If it were true, someone would surely have told her.

"No." Andi shook her head. "That can't be true. I just saw Chad and Melinda. They didn't say anything. Neither did Mitch. They—"

"I wanted to tell you myself," Mother said. "I thought it would be easier for you to hear the news from me." She patted the seat next to her. "Sit down and I'll explain."

Andi backed toward the door. Her heart hammered against the inside of her chest. "You never told me?" It felt impossible to think, like sometimes when she spent too long in the sun. "All these years and you never told—"

"Mamaaa!"

Andi spun around just in time to see a small, brown-haired girl about six years old launch herself through the doorway. The next moment she slammed into Andi, and they went tumbling to the parlor floor.

Behind the screeching girl came a boy a few years older. His face was twisted in fury. He threw himself onto the little girl, who was struggling to right herself.

Andi yelped when the boy's weight fell on her. She grabbed him by his flailing arms and tried to toss him aside, but he was too strong. A fist connected with her chin. She clenched her jaw in pain.

"Levi! Betsy!" Katherine shouted. "Shame on you. Get up this instant."

Neither child paid her the slightest attention but continued to scuffle. Andi was caught in the middle.

Finally, Mother waded into the fray and helped Katherine pull the children apart.

Andi struggled to her feet, breathing hard. Her mind whirled. She glanced from the two howling children to their mother, who looked ready to cry. Andi could understand that. She was close to tears herself.

"Mother, I'm sorry." Melinda appeared in the doorway. A weeping Hannah hung around her neck. "The children got away from me. I didn't mean for them to interrupt you."

Mother crossed the parlor and took the crying toddler from Melinda. "It's all right, darling. These things happen." She turned to Andi. "Why don't we sit down and—"

"No!" Andi shouted over the din. Seeing the shocked look on her mother's face, she took a deep breath. "I mean, I can't right now. I've got to look after Taffy. I left her tied up outside, and Sid told me to take care of her."

She turned and raced from the parlor without waiting for permission to leave. The screaming and hollering put wings to her feet. She didn't stop running until she was out of the house and across the yard.

Andi flung her arms around Taffy and squeezed her neck in a crushing grip. She wanted to scream, but that would draw all kinds of unwanted attention from the busy cowhands. They'd rush over, demanding to know how badly she was hurt—for wasn't that the only fit reason for screaming? When they realized she wasn't snake-bit or bleeding to death, they'd scold her and head back to work.

So Andi clamped her mouth shut and screamed on the inside.
Katherine! My sister? No! It can't be. How could Mother keep such a secret from me? How could the boys and Melinda betray me like this?

Her anger flared. It wasn't easy being the youngest in a busy ranching family. Too often she felt left out of things. But to grow up without knowing she had another sister? That hurt worst of all.

Andi pounded her fist against the saddle. "I've got to find out how this happened." She raised her head and looked back at the house. "I can't go inside. There's too much commotion. Maybe Chad or Mitch?"

She glanced toward the barn and quickly ruled out that option. Her brothers had returned to their important hay harvest. It wasn't likely either of them would drop everything to explain to their baby sister why a missing part of their family had suddenly turned up— no matter *how* sorry Chad had sounded earlier.

"I'll go to town." Andi perked up. She gathered the reins and mounted Taffy, tucking her skirt in around her legs. "Justin will tell me what's going on."

Andi was certain her oldest and favorite brother would be willing to spare a few minutes from his busy schedule to listen to her. Ever since their father had died in a tragic fall from his horse almost seven years ago, Justin had become Andi's confidant and advisor.

Relieved at the opportunity for action, she urged her mare into an easy, loping gait, one Taffy could maintain all the way to town. At that pace, it would take less than an hour to reach Fresno—more than enough time to ponder this new and unasked-for complication in her life. And to think of no less than twenty questions that the appearance of this mystery sister raised.

And to sorely regret giving away her lunch and not having a bite to eat since.

When Andi reached Tulare Street, she tied Taffy to the hitching rail in front of Justin's law office. She stepped up onto the raised wooden sidewalk and paused. Would Justin welcome her this afternoon? Or would he scold her for coming into town on her own, without permission?

"I deserve to be scolded," she muttered. "I didn't tell a soul where I was going." Her long ride into town had also given her time to reflect on what would most likely happen when Mother discovered she'd taken off.

None of her reflections had a happy ending.

"Andi!" Cory clomped up the boardwalk and stopped in front of her. He was breathing hard. "I saw you ride past the livery and figured you were going to see your brother." He gave her a wide grin. "The minute I got home, I asked Pa if he knew who hired the rig out to your place. He told me it was a young woman named Katherine Swanson."

"I know. I met her." She started to brush by him. "I'm in a hurry, Cory. Good-bye."

Cory grabbed her arm. "Hold on, Andi. There's more. She left her baggage at the depot. When she rented the rig, she asked Pa to wait for a message. If she sends word, he's to fetch her luggage from the stationmaster and haul it out to your place. Does that mean she's fixin' to stay awhile?"

"I don't know." *I sure hope not* whispered in her head.

"Who is she?"

Andi felt heat rise to her cheeks. Cory was a good friend, one of her best friends, but she had no intention of telling him her family's secret. Especially when Andi wasn't ready to acknowledge a long-lost sister even to herself. "I really need to see Justin," she said.

"Why won't you tell me?" When Andi pursed her lips and didn't answer, Cory shrugged. "All right, then. Don't tell me. I reckon it's none of my business."

He shoved his hands in his pockets and sauntered off down the boardwalk. "Who cares, anyway?" he threw over his shoulder. Then he turned the corner and disappeared.

Andi slumped. Most days she told Cory all kinds of ranch happenings. He was a good ear when she needed to gripe about Chad's bossiness. He was always the first to learn about a dreaded visit from Aunt Rebecca. Andi had even shared her horrible experience with Chad's wild stallion last spring.

No wonder he acted so hurt. "I'm sorry, Cory," Andi murmured.

She wasn't sorry enough to run after him and spill her news, though. No, sirree! At least not until she'd uncovered the truth about the whole, awful surprise.

Andi took a deep breath, shoved Cory from her mind, and opened the door to her brother's law office.

Justin's outer office and waiting room were large and elegant with polished wood walls, a number of bookshelves, and several pieces of expensive leather furniture resting on a thick carpet. Stained-glass gas lamp fixtures hung over cherrywood tables, where the latest editions of the *Morning Republican* and the *Fresno Weekly Expositor* newspapers lay. The office smelled faintly of rich leather and cigars.

Andi glanced around the room. It was deserted. She tiptoed to Justin's private office and listened. A steady murmur of voices drifted through the heavy, wood-paneled door.

Just before she raised her hand to knock, the door cracked open. Andi jumped back, out of the way. She scrambled over to a waiting chair, threw herself into it, and snatched up the *Expositor*.

"I'll get right on it, Mr. Carter." Tim O'Neil, Justin's clerical assistant, passed through the doorway, his arms full of documents. Reaching out with his free hand, he shut the door and headed to his desk.

Andi put down the newspaper and strolled across the room. "Hello, Tim."

Tim whirled. Papers flew from his arms. He glared at her. "Has no one ever told you it's not polite to sneak up on people?"

"I'm sorry." She crouched and began scooping up the scattered papers. "I'll help you pick up."

"These are important documents, Miss Carter. I'll tend to them." He sighed. "What do you want?"

Andi stood. She surveyed the heap of legal papers at her feet and bit her lip. "I want to see Justin."

Tim returned to his desk, opened a ledger, and ran his finger down the page. "You don't appear to have an appointment."

Andi let out a breath. "I'm his sister. I don't need an appointment."

"I'm afraid you do today," Tim said. "Mr. Carter has a full schedule this afternoon and cannot be bothered with interruptions."

"I'm sure he'll make an exception. At least tell him I'm here."

"I don't suppose you'll leave until I do."

Andi pretended not to hear the clerk's mumbled disapproval. She waited while Tim stepped around the mess on the floor, rapped on the door to Justin's private office, and disappeared inside.

He was back thirty seconds later. "Mr. Carter can give you a few minutes of his time," he said between clenched teeth. "But *only* a few minutes. And please understand that this cannot become a habit, Miss Carter."

"Thank you." Andi hid a smile at Tim's bossy words and hurried into Justin's office.

Justin's private office was half the size of his outer one, but just as richly furnished. The entire back wall consisted of a huge bookcase stacked nearly to the ceiling with law books. Others lay open on his desk. Piles of papers and official-looking documents lay strewn above, below, and around the books.

"Andi!" Justin rose from behind his desk and smiled. "What a pleasant surprise on a dull Saturday afternoon."

"Tim says you're real busy."

"Not so busy that I can't stop and visit with my sister for a few minutes. Did Mother or Melinda come along?" He brought a chair around. "Sit down, honey."

"I"—she fell into the chair—"I came to town alone."

"Oh?" Justin lost his smile. He returned to his desk, sat down, and gave Andi his full attention. "It must be serious."

Andi nodded. "I had to talk to you. It couldn't wait."

"What seems to be the trouble?"

"I want to know about Katherine."

Justin gaped at her.

Andi stared back. She was afraid to say anything more. The look of shock on her brother's face convinced her that she had opened her mouth and made one of the biggest mistakes of her life.

Chapter Five

JOURNEY INTO THE PAST

W ithout a word, Justin rose from his chair and turned to gaze out the window. For a full minute he stood there, hands clasped tightly behind his back, unmoving.

The long silence, and the way her brother remained motionless, frightened Andi. It appeared as if he'd forgotten she was in the room. She groaned inwardly. *Maybe coming to town wasn't such a good idea, after all.*

"I'm sorry, Justin. I didn't mean to upset you or anything." She rose to leave. "I guess I'd better go home."

"What?" Justin spun around. He looked dazed. "No . . . no . . . it's all right."

He returned to his seat and motioned her to sit down. "I'm sorry, but you gave me quite a start. It took me a few moments to collect my thoughts." He smiled. "Why don't we start over? Tell me. What exactly would you like to know about our sister?"

Andi plopped into the chair and stared at her lap. "So, Katherine really is my sister."

"Yes."

Andi sighed. She knew Mother hadn't lied to her, but hearing it from Justin made it real—dreadfully real. For the second time that afternoon, she felt the sting of betrayal. "Nobody ever told me." Her head snapped up. *"You* never told me. Why not?"

"That was Father's decision." Justin sounded regretful.

"Father's decision? But why? Why didn't he want me to know about her?"

Justin took a deep breath and leaned back in his chair. "You were so little—not much more than a baby—and young enough to forget Katherine." He caught Andi's gaze and held it. "It would be best," he suggested softly, "to leave it that way."

"What? Why? What did she do that was so bad?"

"Why are you asking?"

"Mostly because I'm tired of being left out. I'm not a baby any longer, Justin. I'm twelve years old. Old enough to know things about our family, like who this mysterious Katherine is, why she left, and why she's come back."

Justin, who was leaning back in his chair and listening with his usual patience, sat bolt upright. *"What did you say?"*

"I said Katherine's come back. She's out at the ranch, and—"

"Katherine's *here*? At the ranch?" He pushed back his chair and leaped to his feet.

Andi nodded. "Chad acts like he's sorry about something, Melinda's bossing me around, and Mitch squeezed the breath out of me in his excitement. Mother introduced me to Katherine and I"—she cringed at the memory—"I acted like a lunatic and ran out the door. So now Mother's probably upset. Please, Justin. You've got to tell me what's going on."

Again, Justin didn't appear to be listening. He tore across the room and yanked open the door. "Tim, take the rest of the day off. I'm going home."

"Mr. Carter!" Tim glared at Andi, as if he somehow knew this was her fault. "This is the only opportunity you have to catch up on all those—"

"It can't be helped. I'll try to sort through it next week." He grabbed his hat. "Come on, Andi. We're going home."

Her usually composed and levelheaded brother was acting upside down, just like the rest of her family. "But, Justin," Andi protested as she followed her brother out of the office and into the late afternoon sun, "you haven't told me anything."

"I'll tell you on the way home," he promised. "You're right. It's time you learned the Carter family secret."

Andi waited on pins and needles for Justin to keep his promise. The buggy, with Taffy tied securely behind, had left Fresno ten minutes ago, and Andi now simmered with impatience and curiosity.

Just when she thought she might explode, Justin said, "I'm not certain where to begin, or how much Mother wants you to know."

"Pretend you're Father," Andi suggested. "You've been doing that for a long time now. Tell me what he'd say."

"He didn't want you to know *anything*," Justin reminded her.

Andi's heart sank. "All right, then. Tell me where Katherine . . . fits in."

"She comes between Chad and Mitch."

Andi waited for more, but Justin remained quiet. This was not how she imagined him telling her about her unknown sister. "Where has she been for the past"—she turned a questioning look on him— "ten years?"

Justin sighed. "I don't know." He clicked his tongue at the horse and slapped the reins. "Get along, Pal." Pal broke into a fast trot.

Andi bit her lip. Getting Justin to talk about Katherine was proving harder than convincing her mother to let her go on a cattle drive. "Justin," she finally said, "are you going to tell me or not?"

A minute passed. Then Justin took a deep breath and began to speak. He told Andi a story about a little girl who was loved by her parents and adored by her older brothers. He shared happy times— exploring the ranch, racing their horses, and getting in and out of scrapes. He, Chad, and Katherine were as close as any three siblings had a right to be. Mitch was too young to tag along.

"Father called us his 'Three Musketeers' when we were small," Justin said.

Andi couldn't believe her ears. Her big brothers had enjoyed a different life, one she knew nothing about. They had kept it from her all these years. Hot tears stung her eyes.

"She was the only girl for quite a while," Justin went on, "and a spoiled little thing she was. We had fine times together until Katherine began to grow older. Each year she became more self-willed and dissatisfied with the ranch. Nothing made her happy. She hated the dust, the heat, the cattle, and the work. Most of all, she hated living so far from civilization. She'd had a taste of the city, and her heart yearned for the excitement she believed was there."

Andi blinked back her tears. "But, Justin! Town is only an hour away. That's not far."

Justin smiled patiently. "When Katherine was your age, there was no railroad, no Fresno. There was only a little town up in the hills."

"You mean what's left of that old ghost town along the river?"

"That's the one. I'm afraid tiny Millerton couldn't supply Katherine with the social life that she longed for. She wanted to live in San Francisco with Aunt Rebecca. Father said no. Kate was barely fifteen—too young and headstrong to go gallivanting off to the city with only a spinster aunt to look after her. Father knew Rebecca wouldn't be able to control her."

"What happened?"

Justin shrugged. "She went anyway."

"To San Francisco?" Andi was stunned.

Justin nodded. "We didn't know where she'd gone until Aunt Rebecca telegraphed and assured us that Katherine was safe and staying with her." Justin slowed Pal to a walk and turned the reins over to Andi.

"Father was furious, but he gave in and let her stay." Justin leaned back in the buggy. He looked tired and sad. "A few weeks later, another telegram arrived from Rebecca, pleading with us to come get Katherine. She had fallen in with 'unprincipled company'— that's what Aunt Rebecca called it—and she was afraid Katherine would get into trouble. So Father went to San Francisco and brought her home. Kate never forgave him for that."

"This is terrible," Andi whispered.

"Yes," Justin agreed. "And very sad. Katherine was Father's favorite, but they were too much alike, and always clashing. The more he tried to restrain her, the worse she behaved. The house was always in an uproar. Then, suddenly, for a few weeks, Katherine settled down. She started being helpful—playing with you and Melinda, being pleasant at mealtimes. Mother was radiant. She thought her stubborn, self-willed daughter was finally growing up."

"But?" Andi prompted.

"But it was only the calm before the storm. Father didn't realize until too late that Katherine's new attitude was a sham. I think he wanted to believe she'd come around, and we could have some peace at last."

Justin sighed. "Looking back, I should have known better. I knew my sister well. It wasn't like Kate to be so cooperative for no reason. I think I was the only one not surprised when Father discovered that she was secretly meeting with a young man. Worse, he was a man who had a bad reputation with women."

Andi gasped.

"The storm that raged when Father confronted Kate was terrible. I never saw him so angry, frustrated, and helpless as I saw him that day. He didn't know what to do with her. Forbidding her to see Troy would never work, so he locked Kate in her room until he could calm down long enough to talk things over with Mother."

Justin's voice dropped to a whisper. "It was the last time any of us saw her. The next morning we found an open window, an empty room, and a note that said she had the right to live her own life, and she never wanted to see any of us again."

Justin drew a deep breath and finished his sad tale. "When Kate disappeared, she took part of Mother's heart with her and left Father a bitter and broken man. He was in such pain over losing Kate that he refused to allow her name to be spoken. No one argued. It was almost a relief to have her gone. Chad, in particular, didn't care if he ever saw her again. Under all his bluster, our brother has a tender heart. He'd been hurt the most by the turmoil and seemed glad it was finally over."

He paused. "Mother grieved a long time over Katherine, but with God's help our family eventually began to heal. That was ten years ago. We never heard from her, until—apparently—now."

Andi threw aside Pal's reins. "How could she just leave? She had *everything*. How could she be so selfish and hurt Mother and Father like that?"

Justin picked up the reins and cleared his throat. "Before you judge her too harshly, honey, you should take a look at your own actions. You also have everything. Yet last spring you took off and were gone for three long, frightening weeks. Think how that hurt Mother. When she cried for you, she must have wondered if she'd lost you like she'd lost Katherine."

Andi bowed her head in remembered shame. She knew good and well how selfish she felt at times, especially when things weren't going the way she thought they should. This afternoon's unauthorized visit to town was a perfect example. She'd thought only of herself when she'd rushed out of the parlor, mounted Taffy, and run off to see Justin.

She winced. *I'm no better than Katherine.*

Justin nudged her. "Are you all right?"

Andi shook her head. *No, I am not all right*, she wanted to shout. Instead, she raised her head and looked into her brother's face. "Didn't anyone ever think I might want to know about this?"

"As long as Father was alive, no one dared talk about Katherine. After he died, I made an attempt to find her, but it had been too long. She'd disappeared." He picked up one of Andi's hands and squeezed it. "Mother always intended to tell you. She was just waiting until you were a little older. I guess we figured there was no hurry, since it was unlikely Kate would ever return."

He sighed. "I'm sorry, honey."

Andi wasn't quite ready to forgive him. "You're sorry. Chad's sorry. Everybody's sorry, but it doesn't change the fact that I'm always getting left out of things."

Justin didn't reply, and they passed the last few miles home in gloomy silence.

"Justin," Andi said as they pulled into the yard, "why do you suppose she's come home?"

"I have no idea."

"What if she's here to stir up trouble?"

"Don't be silly," he said, bringing Pal to a stop.

Andi caught the slight frown that creased Justin's forehead, and she knew her question wasn't silly. He was clearly thinking the same thing.

Andi wished she'd never heard of Katherine. *Why did she have to come back and throw the family into a muddle?*

When Justin pulled the buggy to a stop, a smiling ranch hand hurried over. "You heard the news, *señor?*" He untied Taffy from the back. "Your sister returns and is up at the house."

Of course, even the ranch hands knew about this missing sister. Everyone knew.

Everyone but Andi.

As quickly as the passing of a summer storm, Justin's worried expression changed to one of excitement and anticipation. "I heard the news, Diego." He climbed from the rig. "Andi rode into town to tell me."

Diego tugged on Taffy's reins. "It is a happy day for the *señora,* no?"

"Indeed it is."

Andi jumped down from the buggy. With a heavy heart, she followed Justin up the steps to the veranda. She wasn't anxious to become acquainted with her new sister, but Justin certainly looked eager. He opened the door and waited for Andi to enter ahead of him.

She glanced around the foyer and sighed in relief. Her mother wasn't waiting to pounce on her for riding off. It gave Andi a few minutes to collect her emotions and think about what she would say when she saw Katherine.

I will be polite for Mother's sake, but nobody can make me like this stranger.

A slow, simmering anger gnawed at Andi's stomach. She wasn't ready to welcome Katherine home with open arms. Because of this selfish, spoiled, older sister's return, Andi's world had turned upside down.

And those three howling kids? Andi's jaw still ached where the boy had punched her.

"Justin, I'm so glad you're home."

Mother glided across the floor with the charm and elegance of a gracious hostess. She could easily have been dressed in a silk evening gown rather than the simple calico work dress and apron she was wearing. Her long, silver-streaked blond hair lay coiled in a neat braid at the nape of her neck.

Justin greeted her with a kiss on the cheek and then sniffed the air. "Must be an applesauce day."

"It was for a while. Luisa and Nila took over." She turned to Andi and frowned. "You've been with Justin?"

Andi nodded.

"That's a relief. You disappeared—again. This must stop, Andrea."

"Yes, Mother. I'm sorry." Andi was secretly relieved at the mild rebuke. It appeared as if her mother had more important things to do at the moment than scold her.

Mother's smile returned. She took Justin's hands and held them tightly. "Andrea told you?"

"I came home as soon as I heard."

"This is a happy day, Justin. The happiest day of my life." She dropped Justin's hands and spun around like a young girl. "Katherine!" she called up the wide stairway. "Justin's home. Andrea too. Come down."

Andi heard the sounds of a door opening and shutting, and then the swishing of a skirt. Melinda appeared and leaned over the balcony railing. "She's coming."

A moment later, Katherine stood at the top of the stairs. Her hair was freshly combed, and she'd changed into a clean dress that Andi recognized as one of Melinda's. Her eyes lit up when she caught sight of their brother. "Justin! You haven't changed a bit."

Justin greeted her with a wide smile. "*You've* changed, Kate. You're prettier than ever. It's good to see you."

Katherine hurried down the stairs and threw her arms around Justin's neck. "You're just as I remember you—so calm, so matter-of-fact. You greet me as if I've been gone ten days instead of ten years. Does nothing ever surprise you?"

Justin returned her embrace. "I must confess, young lady, that your unexpected visit has caught me a bit by surprise."

"Oh, Justin!" Katherine laughed and hugged him tighter. "I've missed you."

Andi watched the affectionate greeting between her brother and sister and felt a stab of jealousy. Justin was *her* brother—her favorite brother. She wasn't ready to share him with a stranger. She felt worse when she remembered that Justin and Katherine had grown up together. Even without hearing Justin's tale, it was easy to see they'd been close.

"Andrea," Mother said quietly, "at least say hello to your sister."

Andi studied the newest family member through narrowed eyes. *Be polite.*

But she couldn't force any words through her tight throat. She didn't want to say hello to Katherine. She didn't want to say *anything* to the young woman who was hugging her brother . . . except good-bye.

And the sooner, the better.

Chapter Six

HOMECOMING

A noisy crash and a shrill cry spared Andi from having to greet Katherine. The same little girl who'd collided with Andi earlier raced along the top of the stairs and leaped onto the banister. Sobbing, she flew down the railing and tumbled to the floor at Andi's feet. Then she picked herself up and stared at Andi. Her cries ceased.

"Betsy!" A shout came from the top of the stairs. "Get back here, you—"

Andi gasped at the string of cuss words that spewed from the dark-haired boy's mouth. She turned to her mother in shock.

Mother's lips were pressed tightly together, but she said nothing.

With a loud whoop, the boy threw himself onto the banister railing. Betsy yelped at the sight. She scurried behind Andi and clung to her skirt.

Oh no! Not again! Andi tried to shake Betsy off. She had no desire to be caught in the middle of another scuffle.

Quick as lightning, Katherine whipped out her hand and snatched the boy by the arm. "Levi! Shame on you. Hush up and leave your sister alone."

Betsy peeked around Andi's skirt, stuck out her tongue at her brother, and called him a name. A *bad* name.

Andi waited, ears burning, to see what her mother or brother would

47

say about this. To her surprise and outrage, Mother ignored Betsy's outburst.

Justin appeared to be following Mother's lead. "Who are these rambunctious, bright-eyed children, Kate?" he asked cheerfully.

Rambunctious children? Andi cringed. *More like foul-mouthed brats.*

Katherine smiled weakly and released her grip on the boy. "This is Levi. He's nine."

Levi scowled. "I'm nearly ten."

"Glad to meet you, young man." Justin held out his hand. "I'm your Uncle Justin." He winked at Andi. "And this young lady who looks just like your mother is your Aunt Andrea. If you want to stay on her good side, however, you'd do well to simply call her Andi."

"We've met," Andi muttered, rubbing her jaw.

Levi shook Justin's hand without speaking. He threw an unfriendly glance in Andi's direction and dismissed her with a shrug.

Katherine sighed. "Say hello, Levi."

"I ain't sayin' hello to no sissy girl."

"I'm sorry," Katherine apologized, red-faced. "It's been a long day." She reached out and drew the little girl from behind Andi. "This is Elizabeth. I named her after Mother."

"I'm *Betsy.*" The child stamped her foot. She shoved her mop of unruly brown tangles from her face and stuck out her tongue at Andi.

"Elizabeth's your real name, sweetie," Katherine reminded her. She ignored her daughter's rude gesture.

Melinda spoke up. "Don't forget Hannah. She's adorable," she told Justin. "She's sleeping right now, but wait 'til you see her. I love her already."

"We'll have a chance to become reacquainted tonight," Mother said. "Supper's at seven. I'll be in the kitchen if you need anything. Luisa, Nila, and I are preparing your favorite dishes, Katherine."

She turned to Andi. "Speaking of supper, I see that it must have been a dusty ride to town. Please change into something suitable for dining. After all"—she turned a tender look on her oldest daughter—"this is a very special occasion." With that, she swept from the foyer.

Katherine's favorite foods? Andi rolled her eyes. *Something suitable for dining?* She glanced down at her calico. It looked clean to her, and more than fitting for eating supper with the family on a Saturday evening.

She threw a helpless look at Melinda, but her sister didn't notice. All her attention was on Justin, Katherine, and the two children.

"You've made Mother happier than I've seen her in a long time, Kate," Justin was saying. "I never realized how much your homecoming would mean to her." He hugged her once more and stepped back. "I think I'll leave you girls to visit, while I catch up on some ranch accounts."

He winked at Katherine. "I'm sure Andi and Melinda would love to hear some wild tales from our childhood. You can start with the time you, Chad, and I decided to do a little gold prospecting up in the hills."

A smile twitched at Kate's lips. "Not *that* story, Justin. It's too—"

"I can't," Andi broke in. She knew exactly what Justin was up to, but it wasn't going to work. No smooth-talking lawyer tricks would persuade her to spend time with her new sister. "I have to change clothes." Suddenly welcoming the excuse to go to her room, she hurried toward the stairs. "I'll see you all at supper."

She wouldn't have thought it was possible to take the stairs *three* at a time, but she did it.

Andi would never forget that first supper with Katherine and her children. The table was set as if they were entertaining the governor of California. The silver had been polished until it sparkled. Everyone was dressed in their Sunday clothes.

The children were scrubbed and their hair freshly combed, thanks to Melinda. From the fussing and yelling that had echoed down the hall, Andi guessed the kids had rarely had a comb taken to their hair, let alone a bath.

While Justin gave a lengthy blessing over the meal, Andi studied her new relatives. None of the children had ever sat at a fancy table before tonight, she decided. It didn't look like they even knew what a prayer was.

Betsy was watching everything with wide, brown eyes. Levi stared sullenly at his place setting. Hannah had snatched a biscuit and was cramming it in her mouth with all the gusto of a starving child.

It wasn't until a platter of roast beef came into her hands that Andi realized Justin must have said "Amen." She was so busy following the antics of her nieces and nephew that she'd been passing dishes along without taking a serving. She speared a piece of meat and sent the platter on to Mitch.

Mitch gave her a puzzled look. "All you're having for supper is one slice of roast beef?"

Andi scowled. "All right, so I'll have *two*." She snagged another slice and slapped it on her plate.

Mitch shrugged and took the platter.

Hannah was seated on Melinda's lap, restless and fussy from her late nap. She refused to eat anything but the biscuits, which she shamefully wasted by scattering pieces all over Melinda's plate, the tablecloth, and the floor.

Halfway through the meal, Hannah reached out to snatch another biscuit and hit the tumbler of milk that sat next to her plate. The liquid splashed onto a serving dish of vegetables and cascaded across the tablecloth.

Like magic, Luisa appeared from the kitchen with a dishtowel to cover the spill. A minute later, she returned with a fresh dish of vegetables, and the meal settled into an uncomfortable silence.

"I'm sorry we're spoiling your special dinner, Mother," Katherine said with a catch in her voice. "The children are exhausted, and frankly, we're not used to living like this."

"I understand," Mother assured her. "It's been quite some time since we've had little ones at the table." She smiled at her grandchildren. "In a few days, I'm sure you'll all be feeling much better."

Betsy yawned and slumped in her chair.

"I asked Nila and her daughter, Rosa, to help with the children for a few days," Mother said. "At least until you're settled in."

Katherine let out a grateful sigh. "Thank you, Mother."

A few minutes later, Rosa and her mother glided into the room. Rosa, smiling and cheerful as ever, helped gather Katherine's children and lead them out of the dining room.

"I don't see why I have to go with the baby girls," Levi protested from the doorway. "I ain't sleepy."

"Don't say *ain't*, son," Katherine said wearily. "It's common."

Levi stamped his foot against the hardwood floor. His eyes snapped with challenge. "Well, I *ain't* sleepy and I *ain't* going with those—" His names for Andi's best friend and her mother were crude and shocking.

Chad pushed back his chair and rose from the table. "You better get something straight right now, boy. We don't put up with that kind of talk around here. Now do what your mother says, and do it quick."

Levi's mouth dropped open. He turned on his heel and scurried after his sisters, but not before tossing out a parting word at his Uncle Chad.

Before Chad could chase him down, Justin raised a hand. "Let it go for now."

Ignore Justin and go after him! Andi wanted to shout.

Levi needed a good talking to, but everybody seemed to be passing over his dreadful behavior. She was disappointed and angry when Chad gave Justin a curt nod and resumed his place at the table.

Katherine turned an apologetic look on the rest of the family. "I'm sorry, Mother. Levi just needs to settle in." She bit her lip. "It seems like I've done nothing but apologize since I got here."

"We understand, Katherine," Mother said. "Don't concern yourself."

"Sure," Mitch put in. "First thing Monday morning I'll get that young cowpoke a mount of his own. Maybe we can wear off some of his energy and bad feelings with a little ranch work."

"Thank you, Mitch."

Mother smiled. "Shall we take coffee and dessert in the parlor?"

"Oh, Mother," Katherine pleaded, "couldn't we stay here? It's been so long since I've sat around the dining room table with my family." A tear trickled down one cheek, quickly followed by another. Soon there was a flood. Katherine covered her face with her hands and sobbed. Her shoulders shook.

"What's wrong, Katherine?" Mother asked in alarm.

Katherine drew a shaky breath and reached for her napkin. "You've all been so kind. You haven't asked me why I've come home after all these years."

"I think we're afraid to find out," Chad said with his usual bluntness, which drew a warning look from Justin.

"I deserved that," Katherine admitted, wiping her eyes. "But the truth is I'm in trouble. I've nowhere to go, and the children need a safe place to stay."

"Where's Troy?" Chad demanded to know.

Katherine shrugged. "I don't know. I haven't seen him in over a year. His crazy schemes usually kept him away from home for weeks, but he always came back. This time I think he's in trouble with the law and can't come home."

"The law?" Melinda squeaked.

"Yes." Katherine shook her head. "You might as well know. I'm so ashamed. I've made my share of mistakes, but Troy was the biggest mistake of all." She sighed. "He was so handsome. Sneaking out to meet him was exciting. He always encouraged me and told me how clever I was."

Katherine's face crumpled. She suddenly looked old and worn out. It was hard for Andi to believe that her sister was only twenty-five. "Believing Troy's lies was the stupidest thing I ever did. I've paid the price in full, and now I've come home to ask your forgiveness. I only wish Father were here so I could tell him how right he was and how sorry I am."

She looked at Andi. "Mother said she never told you about me. It must be an unpleasant surprise to find out that you have a prodigal for a sister." She shrugged. "My return will no doubt set all the loose tongues in town wagging."

That's for sure, Andi agreed silently. Out loud she said, "Things could be better."

"You should have come home years ago," Justin said. "What took you so long?"

Katherine bowed her head. "I really loved Troy, and I thought he loved me. By the time I found out differently, it was too late. I had a baby to think of."

She looked up. Fresh tears glistened at the corners of her eyes. "Troy's nothing but a swindler and a thief. He dragged me all over the country, chasing his ridiculous get-rich-quick schemes. I begged him to let me go home and make things right with my family, but he refused. He told me it was too late, that you'd never take me back, not after what I'd done."

"That's not true," Mother said. Her eyes snapped in anger at Troy's lies.

"Troy said I belonged to him now and I'd better not forget it," Katherine continued. "I was afraid to leave, afraid he'd carry out his threat of hurting me and the children if I ever tried to go home."

The silence around the table grew intense. The coffee turned cold while the family waited to hear the rest of Katherine's story.

Andi swallowed the lump that had suddenly appeared in her throat. She'd heard similar stories before. Sarah Miller's cousin had run away three years ago when the circus came to town. She'd married one of the acrobats, and what a scandal it had caused! Joey Taylor's brother was caught rustling cattle, along with six others, and had been sent to jail.

And of course there was the Hollister clan, shiftless and wild. The oldest girl, Lily, had disappeared last year, only to turn up several months later with a baby in tow. Folks talked about it for weeks.

But Andi had never thought—not in her wildest imagination—that such a shameful thing could happen in her own family. *Just wait 'til the kids at school hear about this. I won't be able to hold my head up.*

Katherine was still talking. "A couple of years ago, Troy disappeared for nearly six months. At first I was glad, because it meant I could settle down and find steady work. Then I discovered he was part of a gang of stagecoach robbers. I was afraid—afraid he'd bring his stolen goods home. I wanted no part of that."

Katherine started to cry. "Troy did come home. And just as I feared, he brought his share of the loot with him. When I told him I wouldn't touch it, he got ugly. He called me horrible names and stomped out of the house. That was a year ago."

Andi groaned inwardly. *I've got a stagecoach robber for a brother-in-law. This is getting worse and worse.*

Katherine shook her head. "It was bad enough knowing that Troy made a living out of swindling folks, but *this*! I knew I had to get away and start a new life—for my children's sake—before it was too late."

She dabbed her eyes with a napkin. "It took me nearly a year to save the money for train fare, and then I worried the entire trip west. What if you didn't want to see me? God knows I don't deserve any sort of welcome for the way I treated you."

Katherine shivered and glanced around the table with pleading eyes. "When Troy returns to Chicago and discovers I've left, he'll be furious. He'll hunt me down."

She paused and drew a deep breath. "I hope you'll let me stay for a week or two, until I can figure out where I will go. If that's too much to ask, I'll leave tomorrow. But would you . . . might you . . . be willing to keep the children for a while? They would be safe here, of that I'm certain. I'd come back for them when I know Troy is gone for good."

"Of course you'll stay," Justin said. "You *and* your children, for as long as you like." He pushed back his chair and stood up. "I don't know about the rest of the family, but I know what Father would say if he were alive."

Andi watched Justin carefully. What *would* Father say if he were here?

"He'd say, 'Bring the fatted calf, and kill it; and let us eat and be merry. For this my . . . *daughter* . . . was dead, and is alive again; she was lost, and is found.'"

Justin opened his arms and smiled. "Welcome home, Kate."

Chapter Seven

RETURN TO THE CREEK

"Why are you always following me around?" Andi asked her nephew a few days later. She settled the saddle onto Taffy's back and started to cinch it up.

"It's a free country," Levi shot back. He laid his hand on the palomino's rump. "Where're you going?"

"Riding."

"Where to?"

"Up to my special spot along the creek." Andi threaded the strap through the ring and gave it a yank. "If that means anything to you."

"It doesn't. Why're you going there?"

"If you *must* know, I'm taking a few supplies to a poor fellow Cory, Rosa, and I rescued last week from being buried alive in mud."

Levi's face lit up. "Really? I wanna come."

"You can't."

"Why not?"

Andi lost her temper. "Because I'm tired of you tagging along wherever I go." She didn't dare tell Levi the real reason—that she didn't trust him not to blab about TJ to the rest of the family.

Andi had managed to slip away after school one other day this week, with a grub sack for the unfortunate stranger. She'd even managed to snag him a wide-brimmed hat to keep the sun off his head. TJ had been pleased to see her and said so. Andi figured this one last supply trip would be enough to assure herself that TJ could now fend for himself and go on his way with no worries.

Levi gave Andi a scheming look. "If you don't let me go, I'll tell Grandmother what you're up to."

"You better not!"

"Then take me with you. I can ride. Uncle Mitch gave me Patches for my very own."

Andi bit back the angry reply that leaped to her lips. *You don't deserve a pony.*

Mitch's gift to Levi annoyed her, as did all the attention her brother was heaping on their horrid nephew. He'd spent hours teaching Levi to ride, and boasted to anyone who would listen what a good rider the boy was.

What's more, Mitch had redone Levi's chores all week.

When Andi pointed out that Levi should do his own chores, Mitch had grinned and said, "I've done *your* chores plenty of times, Sis. Why shouldn't I lend a hand to Levi?" There was truth in her brother's words, but it irritated Andi all the same.

Scowling at the memory, Andi finished saddling Taffy. "You can't come," she told Levi. She dropped the stirrup in place, grabbed the reins, and pulled herself into the saddle. "You can go with me another time," she relented, seeing the hurt look on Levi's face. "I'm in a hurry today."

Indeed, if Andi wanted to make it to the creek and back before the sun set, she'd have to hustle. There was never enough time after school to ride, and the short fall days cut deeply into this pleasure. Without waiting for a response from Levi, she urged Taffy into a lope and headed for the hills.

Free at last! Andi rejoiced at the few minutes of peace and privacy she planned to enjoy on her ride up to her special spot.

It had been a dreadful week, and watching Mitch and Levi together was only a small part of it. Adjusting to new family members was a lesson Andi wasn't learning well. It had taken her only a few days to realize that having her oldest sister—and especially the three children—on the ranch would be the biggest challenge of her life.

Her cheeks burned when she recalled Justin's tongue-lashing from the day before. She'd been in a particularly sour mood on the ride home from school and had poured out her complaints without thinking . . .

"It's 'Katherine this' and 'Katherine that.'" Andi crossed her arms and slouched against the back of the buggy. "Would you like to go riding this afternoon, Katherine?" She mimicked her mother's gentle voice. "Diego can saddle Snowflake for you. I'll have him saddle Champ for me." "Katherine, shall we go into town today and visit the dressmaker? She has some lovely silks just in from San Francisco."

Andi clenched her teeth in frustration. "Every time I try to talk to Mother, she has one of those whiny little girls on her lap. I can't finish a sentence without being interrupted. Worse, they follow me around wherever I go. And Levi! You should have heard the name he called me—"

"That will be just about enough from you."

If Justin had slapped her, Andi would not have been more surprised. She jerked her head around. "But Justin—"

"I know you've been out of sorts lately," Justin continued, "and I don't blame you. You were hurt to find out about Katherine so suddenly. I'm sorry. That's our fault. However"—he fixed a stern look on her—"it's over. Katherine is your sister, and she'll be staying at the ranch for as long as she wants. So will the children. You will stop this petty complaining and try to be a little understanding. Do I make myself clear?"

Shocked into silence, Andi nodded and kept quiet the rest of the way home.

Even now, on her way to the creek, Justin's scolding cast a shadow over her pleasant ride. She scowled, shook herself free of her musing, and urged Taffy into a gallop.

Half an hour later, she topped a small rise and came into view of her favorite spot on the ranch. TJ Silver lifted his arm in welcome. He was standing with his large bay gelding, next to what was left of the creek. When Andi drew near, he called out a greeting.

"Howdy yourself!" Andi reined Taffy to a stop and dismounted. "Look at you! You're up and around, good as new."

TJ removed his hat and bowed. "Thanks to you, I feel like a new man. Those hearty sandwiches and a chance to rest without worrying about being chased down did the trick." He smiled. "Seriously, Andi, I don't know how I can ever repay you. You and your friends most likely saved my life the other day."

His gratitude warmed Andi clear through. "You don't have to repay me. I was happy to help." She reached out and tugged at the sack of food tied to her saddle horn. "I'm sure you'd do the same for me," she added, handing over the supplies.

TJ took the grub sack and tossed it to the ground. "Hard to say. Where I come from, folks aren't so quick to lend a hand. Too many ruffians around to rob 'em when their backs are turned."

Andi paused and took a long, hard look at her new friend. She sure hoped *he* wasn't one of those ruffians he was talking about. He certainly looked the part, though, with his wild hair and the scraggly growth on his face.

It suddenly dawned on her that Cory was right. She knew nothing about Mr. TJ Silver. "Where are you from?" she asked. "And what are you doing here?"

TJ ran his fingers through his brown tangles and replaced his hat. For a moment, his eyes darkened. "Where I come from, folks don't ask a lot of pesky questions."

Then he chuckled. "Don't worry, Andi. I'm not going to rob you. Where am I from? East of the Mississippi. What am I doing here? Looking for work. Do you know of any spreads needing an extra hand?"

Andi smiled in relief. "Sure! Our ranch. There are always fences to mend or posts to be cut. I'm sure our foreman Sid could find you work, at least until you're ready to—"

TJ's attention shifted to something behind her. "Say, Andi. Who's your friend?"

Andi turned and shaded her eyes. A small figure on a sharp-looking paint horse was galloping over the rise. *Levi followed me!*

She groaned. "It's my nephew. He won't leave me alone."

TJ pulled his hat over his forehead, folded his arms across his chest, and grinned. "Nephew? You don't look old enough to be an aunt."

Andi cringed. She hated being called aunt. Furious at Levi for invading her special spot, she took off running to meet him. "Don't bother to dismount," she called when he pulled up beside her. "Just hightail it back to the ranch this minute."

Levi tossed the reins aside and slid off his horse. "You're not my boss." He pointed at TJ, who was bent over, checking his horse's feet. "Is that the poor fella you rescued?"

"Never mind," Andi snapped. "You get back on that horse and go home. Right now."

Levi paid her no mind. He took two steps toward TJ.

Andi caught his sleeve. "You mount up and get back to the ranch or I'll tell Chad you're not taking proper care of Patches. You might have Mitch wrapped around your little finger, but you can't fool Chad."

Her words stopped Levi in his tracks. It was obvious he preferred to steer clear of his tall, short-tempered uncle. Chad had no patience with sloppy or unfinished chores.

Levi jerked away from Andi's grasp. "All right. I'll leave." He mounted Patches. "But—"

"But what?"

He bit his lip. "I'm not sure how to get home."

Andi sighed her impatience. As much as she wished Levi would go away, she didn't want him to wander around this vast rangeland alone. He could easily get lost. "Fine. I'll go with you."

Annoyed at how Levi had managed to wrangle his own way, Andi returned to the creek and grabbed Taffy's reins. "I'd better head back," she told TJ, "before somebody wonders what happened to Levi."

TJ straightened up. "Thanks for the supplies. This should get me by a couple more days. Then I'll check with that foreman of yours . . . Sid?"

"Sid McCoy," Andi said, mounting her horse.

"Much obliged. I'll see you around." He waved and returned to his careful examination of his horse.

Andi nudged Taffy and called to Levi. "Let's get going. If somebody comes looking for us, we'll both be in trouble."

With a shrug of apparent indifference, Levi gathered up the reins. He turned a sly look on Andi and smirked. "Whenever you're ready, Auntie Andi."

Chapter Eight

A HANDFUL OF NIECES

A ndi fumed most of the way back to the ranch. *Auntie Andi indeed!* She knew Levi called her that just to annoy her, and it worked every time. She glanced behind her shoulder to make sure he was keeping up.

"Wanna race?" he yelled.

Andi wanted to refuse, but she couldn't pass up an opportunity to race. She waited until Levi caught up and then gave him a curt nod.

With an ear-splitting Indian war cry, the boy slammed his heels into his paint horse and took off like a shot. Andi gulped back her surprise, tightened her hold on the reins, and urged Taffy into a gallop.

Catching Levi would be a challenge. He clung to his horse like a burr, shouting his encouragement and shrieking with laughter. Patches responded by giving his rider his all. It was nothing short of amazing, considering Levi's first ride on a horse had occurred less than a week ago.

Andi hadn't realized the paint horse was so fast. With Levi's spur-of-the-moment head start, she would have a hard time winning this race. "Come on, Taffy," she urged her mare. "We can't let a nine-year-old greenhorn beat us."

He almost did. Andi barely managed to finish the race with a tie. "Nice race," she admitted when they were cooling down their mounts.

"Next time I'm gonna beat you," Levi bragged.

"You can try," Andi said with a grin. "But no more head starts."

He laughed. His earlier anger toward Andi seemed to have dissolved. "I'll beat you with or without a head start."

"We'll see about that."

Together, they trotted into the yard and dismounted. Levi led Patches into his stall.

Andi entered Taffy's stall to rub down her horse. Her eyes widened to find Betsy crouched in a corner. *What in the world?*

"I been waiting for hours and hours," the little girl said in an exasperated voice.

"What for?"

Betsy scrambled to her feet. "For you. I wanna help." She snatched up a brush, scurried underneath Taffy, and began attacking the mare's underbelly with quick, careless strokes. Taffy quivered and flicked her ears.

"Get out from under there, before you get stepped on."

Betsy crawled out and stood up. "I wanna help."

Andi sighed. "All right." She took the brush from Betsy and showed her how to groom the mare properly. Less than five minutes later, the little girl was under Taffy again, brushing her belly and poking at her.

"Betsy, I told you to stay out from under there."

Betsy tossed the brush to the ground. "I'm done brushing." She made her way around to Taffy's backside. "I'm gonna braid her tail and make it pretty." She grabbed two fistfuls of the stiff, ivory-colored hair.

Before Andi could stop her, Betsy yanked. Taffy whinnied and shied away, slamming into Andi and pinning her against the side of the stall.

Andi gasped at the crushing pain. Tears sprang to her eyes. She slapped her horse and gritted her teeth. "Move over." Wriggling away from the huge golden body, she clutched her aching ribs and rounded on Betsy. "Get away from my horse."

Betsy hung on tighter. "No. I wanna make Taffy look pretty."

"You're going to get us stomped on!" Kind words would go further with Betsy than hollering, but Andi hurt too much to be patient. All she wanted to do was sink down in the hay and catch her breath.

She couldn't. Taffy was growing more and more agitated. "Let go of her tail and get out of here. *Now!*"

Betsy didn't move. Andi reached for her, but Betsy scuttled out of the way, still clutching Taffy's tail.

Taffy tossed her head. She laid her ears back and danced nervously.

Andi caught Betsy's arm and yanked her away just as Taffy lashed out with a hind foot. It narrowly missed them both. As it crashed against the stall's back wall, the sound of splintering wood filled the air.

"Now see what you've done!" Andi dragged Betsy across the stall. With her free hand, she fumbled for the latch until it slipped aside. Then she opened the stall's half door and pushed the little girl through the opening. "Get out and stay out."

Betsy tripped and landed in the aisle. An instant later she was on her feet, rubbing grubby fists in her eyes. She stamped her foot. "I'm gonna tell my mama on you! You're mean and ugly! Your horse stinks!"

Her voice rose until her words gave way to high-pitched screeching. Each shriek was accompanied by a wild kick in Andi's direction.

"Hey!" Andi skipped out of the way and slammed the half door shut between them. Betsy screamed louder.

"What on earth is going on here?" Chad shouted over the commotion. He made his way to Taffy's stall. Betsy was beating her fists against the door. "Good grief, Andi, what did you do to her? We can hear her screeching clear across the yard."

"I told her to leave. She nearly got us both kicked."

Chad turned his attention to Betsy. "Stop that howling and go find your mother."

Betsy shrank at Chad's rebuke, gulped back a sob, and tore out of the barn.

Andi rested her arms across the half door. "Thanks for the help." She gave Chad a grateful smile. After Justin's scolding yesterday, it felt good to think that at least one brother seemed sympathetic to her frustrations.

Chad grinned and ruffled her hair. "My pleasure."

Just as quickly, her brother lost his smile. "I don't know why Kate doesn't make those kids behave. They're wild little things. Half the time they're bold as brass, and the rest of the time they act scared of their own shadows."

He gave Andi an understanding look. "I know you're having trouble adjusting to Kate's return. If you need to get off by yourself for a little peace and quiet sometime, let me know. I'll find something for you to do away from the house."

"Thanks. I'll remember that." Andi hung over the door and watched her brother leave. Then with a sigh of relief, she returned to her chores. She glanced at the gaping hole in the wall and winced. "Good thing Chad didn't see this," she murmured, giving Taffy a pat. "Maybe I'll ask one of the hands to fix it before he finds out."

That decided, Andi gently combed out Taffy's tail, apologizing for the rough treatment the mare had received. "I wish I could stay longer, but it's getting late. I've got to get back inside and help with supper." She hugged Taffy, dumped a measure of oats into her feeder, and left.

It wasn't hard to find a sympathetic ranch hand to mend Taffy's stall, and Andi felt relieved as she headed for the back door.

Mother was waiting for her inside. "What happened in the barn, Andrea? Betsy ran into the house, sobbing at the top of her lungs."

Andi crossed to the sink and shoved her hands under the kitchen pump. She grabbed the soap and said, "She pulled Taffy's tail and got me smashed against the stall. Then Chad came in and told her to go find her mother." Andi dried her hands and looked around. "Where is she?"

"In the parlor with Kathetine. She's trying to comfort her. You didn't hit Betsy, did you?"

Andi's eyes opened wide. "Of course not. But I did drag her out of Taffy's stall. I wasn't gentle about it, either." She tossed the towel aside. "And I guess I yelled at her too. I'm sorry."

Mother sighed. "I know this has been a difficult adjustment for you, sweetheart. It takes some getting used to, having younger children around the house."

Andi remembered Justin's warning and bit off a quick retort before it could find its way out of her mouth. "I know. I just wish . . ." Her voice trailed off.

"What do you wish?"

"The honest truth?"

Mother nodded.

"Everything's turned upside down since Katherine's come home. I wish she . . . she . . ." Andi fumbled for words.

"You wish she'd never come home?" Mother finished.

Andi dropped her gaze and nodded. She felt her face grow hot.

Mother pulled Andi into a tender hug. "I know Katherine must seem like a complete stranger to you. Please try to remember that she was once a little girl like you, and I love her as much as I love you. I want her to feel comfortable staying on the ranch for as long as she wants, until things settle down for her and the children. Can you be patient?"

"I don't know." Andi unwound her arms from around her mother's waist. "But I'll try," she promised.

"That's all I ask," Mother said. "Now go change and then set the table for supper."

Andi's noble intention to show patience toward her sister's family dissolved the instant she entered her bedroom to change clothes. She stifled a scream at the sight before her.

The room looked as if an earthquake had struck. The bed was rumpled and unmade. Dirty footprints danced across the quilt and onto the floor. A shelf containing her collection of favorite books was empty, the books scattered across the room like jackstraws.

With a low moan, Andi explored the devastation. The top of her dresser was strewn with the contents of her treasure box. Marbles, a small gold nugget, a small photograph of her family, and other prized items were scattered and damaged.

Andi picked up a necklace made from tiny shells—a gift from an Indian girl she'd met years ago. She had been six years old and scared to death of Indians until she and her friend Riley had met people from the Yokut tribe, who lived in a far corner of the Circle C ranch.

After a short stay with the Yokuts, the little girl had offered to trade her necklace for Andi's red hair ribbon. Both had departed content, with not one English or Yokut word passing between them.

Choo-nook's necklace now looked as if someone had banged it against the floor. A dozen shells were chipped or missing. Andi looked around for the pieces, but the damage was done.

She found her treasure box upside down on the floor. She scooped it up with one hand and carefully laid the broken necklace inside. Then she gathered up the rest of her collection.

She paused a moment to shake the huge rattle from the snake Mitch had killed up in the hills six summers ago. He'd brought the rattle home just for Andi, claiming it was the largest snake he'd ever seen.

Thankfully, the delicate scales of the rattle appeared undamaged. She set it next to the necklace.

As she gathered up the rest of her treasures—the gold nugget, a dozen agate marbles, a bullet Cory insisted came from the leg of an old Yankee soldier he'd met—Andi's thoughts buzzed like a swarm of angry bees. Who would dare rummage through her things? Who would enter her bedroom without permission?

"I bet it was Levi." She rolled up the dirty quilt and dropped it on the floor. "I'll pay him back for this. I really will." Then she paused. When would Levi have had time to wreck her room? Mitch was keeping him busy around the ranch.

"Hi, Nandi," a tiny voice piped up.

Andi spun around.

In the doorway stood Hannah, her golden curls sticking up everywhere, her face flushed from sleep. She was clutching a battered rag doll.

Andi caught her breath in sudden realization. Hannah had destroyed her room. Only a three-year-old could have torn things apart so completely and jumped on her bed with such abandon. Hannah would think nothing of exploring a box of treasures and then tossing it to the floor in boredom.

"See my pretty dolly." Hannah held up her doll for Andi to see. She popped her thumb in her mouth and waited for a response.

Andi stared, speechless. Around the doll's neck hung the locket Justin had given Andi for her tenth birthday. It was a costly gift, fashioned from gold and etched with tiny swirls. Engraved on the back in fine script were the words "May you grow in wisdom and God's grace, sweet sister." Even more precious were the miniature portraits of Mother and Father the locket held inside.

Andi's anger burned quick and hot. It was bad enough that Hannah had touched the necklace from Choo-nook, but *this*! She exploded. "Give me my locket!"

Hannah's cornflower blue eyes filled with tears. She removed her thumb and set up a wail. "*My* lecklace." She grasped the locket in her chubby hand. "Mine."

Andi took a step toward her little niece. "It's *not* yours. It's mine, and you took it. You also destroyed my room and got into my things."

Hannah turned tail and ran. She rushed to the top of the stairs, sobbing. Andi followed and snatched her up before the tiny girl could tumble down the stairs. She tucked Hannah under her arm and sailed down the staircase.

"Mother!" She stormed into the kitchen, a howling Hannah still under her arm.

Melinda, with a now-quiet Betsy sitting beside her at the table, looked up in surprise.

Katherine rushed over. "What happened?" She pulled Hannah from Andi's arms. "Shh, darling. It's all right. Did you wake up from your nap frightened?"

Hannah clung to her mother and sobbed. "Mine!"

"Andrea?" Mother raised her eyebrows in confusion. "Do you know why she's carrying on?"

"You bet I do. Hannah tore my room apart and jumped all over my bed with her dirty feet. Worst of all, she took the locket Justin gave me." A pang of fear stabbed Andi. "She's going to break it."

"How could she have done that?" Katherine asked. "She's been asleep."

"I guess she wasn't as asleep as you thought," Andi snapped. She reached for Hannah's doll. Hannah shrieked.

Katherine sat down and cradled Hannah in her lap. "Let me see Tessie, sweetie." The little girl tearfully held out the doll for her mother's inspection.

Katherine's face reddened at the sight of the locket. She carefully removed it and dropped it into Andi's waiting hands. "I'm so sorry, Andi. I put her to bed right after the noon meal. She must have gotten up and done some exploring before going to sleep." She bit her lip. "Is there much damage?"

Andi didn't answer right away. She clicked open the locket. To her great relief, her parents' miniatures were still firmly in place. She closed the locket and fastened it securely around her neck. *The only safe place in the house.*

Her anger cooled at her sister's heartfelt apology. "Things are mostly scattered all over the place," she told Katherine in a quieter tone. "The quilt will have to be washed. Her footprints are all over it."

Katherine lifted Hannah's chin. "You have been very naughty, Hannah. You mustn't go into Andi's room."

Hannah looked forlornly at the empty neck of her doll. Then she glanced at Andi. Her lower lip quivered, and she whimpered. "*My lecklace.*" She reached for the locket hanging around Andi's neck.

"No, Hannah. It's Andi's necklace. You must tell her you're sorry."

Hannah put her thumb in her mouth and looked down into her mother's lap. She shook her head. When Katherine attempted to remove her small daughter's thumb, she howled.

"It's all right, Katherine." Andi suddenly felt like a scoundrel for making Hannah unhappy. "Could you please just keep her out of my room?"

Katherine nodded. "I'll watch Hannah more closely. Would you like me to go up and straighten your room?"

Andi was strangely moved by her sister's humble words. "No. I'll clean it myself. You don't know where anything goes." She smiled at Katherine. "Thanks just the same."

"Andi?" Betsy jumped up and took hold of Andi's hand. "Can I help you? Please? I'm sorry I pulled Taffy's tail and said mean things to you."

Andi glanced down into Betsy's pleading brown eyes. She felt the little girl's small, warm hand clasp hers in eagerness. "All right. You can help me. And if you do a good job and promise to mind me when we're around Taffy, I'll let you look inside my secret box."

"A truly secret box?" Betsy's eyes grew wide.

Andi grinned at the awe on Betsy's face. She nodded. "Have you ever shaken a rattlesnake's rattle?"

Betsy shook her head. "Will it bite?"

Andi couldn't help it. She laughed. "No, silly. It's the rattle of the snake, not the mouth." She gave Betsy's hand a tug. "Come on."

Betsy beamed her delight. She squeezed Andi's hand and whispered, "I like you, Andi. I really, really do."

Andi felt the hard shell around her heart crack—just a little.

Chapter Nine

TROUBLE IN THE SCHOOLYARD

"This is my nephew, Levi Swanson," Andi announced at school the following Monday. Katherine had decided that Levi had adjusted to the ranch, so he should now settle into school for the final weeks before the holidays.

Neither Andi nor Levi received the news with joy. "He's staying out at the ranch for a while," she explained to Levi's teacher.

There were a few muffled giggles at this. Andi pressed her lips together. Everybody in Fresno—including the schoolchildren— knew who was staying at the Circle C and why. It hadn't taken long for word to spread about the mysterious return of a long-lost sister of questionable reputation.

It made for great gossip around town. Andi especially dreaded Sunday mornings, when the folks at church spent more time staring at her family and whispering than listening to the preacher.

"Welcome, Levi," Miss Hall said cheerfully. "How old are you?"

"Almost ten."

Miss Hall recorded his name and age in the roll book and glanced up. "Now, where shall I seat you?"

Toby Wright waved an eager hand in the air. "He can sit with me, Miss Hall. Frankie took sick last week and won't be back before the holidays."

"Fine. Have you any books, Levi?"

"Yes'm. My aunt gave me some of her old ones." The class tittered. "What's so funny?" he demanded. "Andi *is* my aunt, so there!"

"That's true, Levi. And you couldn't have a nicer one." Miss Hall smiled until Andi felt squirmy all over.

"Thank you, *Auntie Andi*, for helping me find my class." The look in Levi's eyes mocked her.

The class howled with laughter. Levi smirked.

"Just see if I help you with anything else," Andi hissed in Levi's ear. "Now go sit down and don't give Miss Hall any trouble."

Levi responded by shoving Andi aside and stomping off to his new seat beside Toby.

As Andi left the classroom, she heard Toby chattering away. "You're lucky to have Andi for an aunt, Levi. She's the nicest girl in the whole school, and she plays ball near as good as the big boys. I wish she was *my* aunt."

Levi grunted a reply that sounded like, "You can have her."

Andi shook her head and headed for the stairs that led up to her classroom. She wished there was something she could find to like in her ornery, smart-mouthed nephew. Except when they were racing their horses, Levi acted like he had no use for her. Yet he followed her around from dawn 'til dusk, pestering her until she wanted to clap a hand over his mouth.

Levi was ill-mannered and foul-mouthed, always ready to start a fight over the smallest offense. The only person he appeared to respect and truly like was Mitch. He never talked about his father.

"You could have told me Katherine Swanson is your sister."

Cory's words yanked Andi from her thoughts. She looked up.

Cory crossed his arms over his chest and gave her a hurt look. "That day in town, remember? You could have told me. Instead, I had to find out from the town busybodies." He dropped his arms to his sides. "I thought we were friends."

Andi didn't know what to say. She'd been so caught up in her own misery the past couple of weeks that she'd hardly noticed Cory, much less talked to him at school. "I'm sorry," she muttered.

Cory clearly wasn't finished with her. "And another thing. Whatever happened with that suspicious-looking fella up at the creek? I suppose you took him supplies? By yourself, I bet."

"So what if I did? TJ's not suspicious-looking. He's friendly, and very grateful for our help. I told him to ask Sid for a job."

Cory opened his mouth to reply, but just then the bell rang. He and Andi exchanged a look of panic and clattered up the steps, forgetting their disagreement for the time being.

"Miss Carter. Mr. Blake." The schoolmaster pierced them with a look when they rushed into the classroom. "The tardy bell has found you out of your seats."

"I'm sorry, Mr. Foster." Andi slid into the double seat she shared with Rosa. "I had to show my nephew his class and introduce him to Miss Hall. I didn't mean for it to take so long."

"And your excuse, Mr. Blake?"

Cory gave the teacher an innocent smile. "I was seeing Miss Carter safely up the stairs."

There were a few snickers, which Mr. Foster cut short. "I see." He kept his face a mask, but his eyes showed his amusement. "I will suspend the consequences for being tardy this time, because you were assisting a new student. But tomorrow . . ." He let the unspoken warning hang in the air.

"Yes, sir," Andi and Cory replied together.

"Andi!" someone shouted during recess. "Come quick!"

Andi froze. The jump rope slapped against her ankles and sent her to the ground with an unladylike *thud*. "Ouch!"

"*Lo siento,*" Rosa apologized, dropping the rope. "It happened so fast."

"It's all right." She rose and dusted off her skirt.

"Andi!" The shout came again, this time accompanied by the sounds of a scuffle.

Toby ran up and grabbed her hand. His eyes were wide with alarm. "Hurry! Levi's fighting Jacob Powers."

"Oh no!" Andi raced after Toby and found the boys rolling in the dust. She arrived just in time to hear Levi swear at Jacob and call him a name that made Andi flush in anger and embarrassment. "Levi! Jacob! Stop it!"

Both boys ignored her. Jacob was hollering and thrashing and sobbing, but Levi refused to back off. His fist crashed into Jacob's red face.

Fear gripped Andi. Jacob was no match for Levi. He was the only child of Matthew Powers, an attorney in town and Justin's friend and colleague. Mr. Powers set great store by his small son and would certainly take offense at Levi's attack.

How in the world had Levi gotten himself into such a fix?

Andi didn't stand still wondering for long. She took a deep breath and waded into the scuffle. To her surprise and relief, Cory joined her. He rescued Jacob from under Levi, leaving the bigger boy to Andi.

She gripped Levi by his shoulders and gave a yank that sent him sprawling. "Stop it!"

Levi leaped up and threw himself toward Jacob again. Cory backed away, pulling Jacob with him. He deflected Levi's blow with his free arm and pushed him aside. "Quite a nephew you've got there, Andi. A real wildcat."

Andi ignored Cory. She reached for Levi, who was shouting at Jacob, "Come back here, you little—"

Just in time, Andi clapped her hand over Levi's mouth. He responded by slamming an elbow into her stomach and prying her hand away. "Let me go. It's my fight."

Andi didn't let go. She didn't dare. She set her jaw, ignored the pain in her belly, and hung on to Levi as a curious crowd gathered around them.

By the time Miss Hall and Mr. Foster arrived, things had settled down. The schoolmaster frowned at Levi. "You, sir, will explain the meaning of this."

Levi shook himself free of Andi's grip and wiped a sleeve across his bloody nose. "That low-down, stinkin—" He caught himself, saw Andi glaring at him, and bit his lip. "That sniveling baby accused me of swiping his marbles. I didn't."

"You *did* steal them," a soft voice piped up.

Jacob stood beside Cory, a handkerchief to his nose. One eye was already turning black and blue. His shirt was torn, and a thick coat of dust covered his britches. "If you look in his pocket, you'll find my best aggie and two steelies. I want them back."

Andi thrust her fingers into the pocket of Levi's overalls. He stood still as a statue, watching her. She withdrew her hand and uncurled her fingers. Three shiny marbles gleamed up from her palm. She lifted the marbles to Levi's face. "What are these, Levi?"

"I won 'em. Fair and square. But this baby boy is too stingy to admit it."

"That's not true," Jacob said. "Ask Toby. Ask anybody. When my back was turned, Levi snatched the marbles from the circle and ran off."

Levi turned to Andi. "I did not!" His lip quivered. "It's because I'm new here. It always happens. Nobody ever believes me. They all gang up on me and make fun of me, just cuz I don't have no pa." Two large tears fell from his eyes.

There was a sudden, sympathetic murmur from Miss Hall. "Poor little thing."

Andi glanced past Levi and saw Toby shaking his head. Frowning, she stepped away from her nephew. "Don't waste your tears on me, Levi. You took the marbles." She was so angry and confused that she wanted to slap him. Instead, she clutched the marbles until her fingernails dug into her palm. "Didn't you?"

Levi's wounded look turned sullen. "So what if I did?"

Andi turned her back on Levi and walked stiffly over to Jacob. "Here are your marbles, Jacob. I'm sorry Levi took them. I'm sure his mother will speak to him about it."

But Andi *wasn't* sure. She'd discovered early on that Katherine seemed afraid to discipline her children. Whether she felt sorry for them or whether she didn't know how to handle their misbehavior, Andi couldn't tell.

Mr. Foster clearly had no such misgivings. He turned to Miss Hall. "With your permission, ma'am, I will thrash this unruly young pupil of yours, in order to teach him not to lie and steal and fight."

Miss Hall looked at Levi and shook her head. "Not today, Mr. Foster, although I appreciate your offer. I think for Levi's first day of school we will temper justice with mercy." Her look turned stern. "I insist, however, that you apologize to Jacob."

Levi stuck out his lower lip and muttered a clipped apology. Then he shuffled back to the schoolhouse, head bowed.

Jacob sniffed back his tears and looked at Andi. "When Papa sees my face, he's going to be mighty upset. He'll want to know how it happened."

Andi watched Levi enter the schoolhouse. "I reckon."

"I'll have to tell him." Jacob sounded regretful.

"I guess your father will be calling on my sister."

"Yep," Jacob said softly. Then he hurried away to join his friends.

Andi felt drained. She started back to class, too tired to return to her rope jumping. What would Mother say when she found out about Levi's fight? Would she wonder why Andi hadn't prevented such a scene?

"Probably," she muttered, kicking a rock. Somehow, she knew Levi's troubles would soon become her own.

Chapter Ten

MORE TROUBLE

A ndi and Levi crouched side by side on the second-story landing. They pressed their faces against the balcony railing and struggled to hear the conversation coming from the parlor below them and out of sight.

"Jacob's pa looked mighty fired up when Grandmother invited him in," Levi whispered. "Do you suppose Mama will ask Uncle Justin to switch me?"

Andi hesitated before answering. "I don't know. Justin's real patient most times, but I suppose if Mr. Powers insists, he'll probably have to do it. After all, you pounded Jacob pretty good."

Levi cringed and squeezed his eyes shut. Tears oozed between his eyelids and trickled down his cheeks.

Andi laid a gentle hand on his shoulder. Suddenly, he didn't seem so much a pest, only a scared little boy. "Maybe your mother will do it herself."

Levi shook his head and brushed a hand across his cheek. "She won't. She never does. I guess she figures Pa thrashed me enough for the both of 'em."

Andi swallowed her uneasiness at Levi's words. Against her will, she whispered, "Why?"

Levi glanced up. "Why what?"

"Why did your father whip you?"

"That's Pa," he replied, as if it made perfect sense. "Lots of things riled him." He shrugged. "'Specially when he had too much to drink."

"But—"

"Hush!" Levi nudged her. "Don't you want to hear what they're saying?"

The two returned to their eavesdropping.

Andi glanced at Levi from the corner of her eye. Her heart thumped against the inside of her chest as she considered his words. No wonder he was afraid. She wondered how Levi had come to deserve such a fate. Sure, he was a pest, but—

"Hey! What're you doing?" Betsy's piping voice shattered the silence, and Andi's thoughts.

"Shh!" Levi reached out and pulled his sister to the floor. "You've got a mouth like a hippopotamus."

Betsy responded with a shriek that pierced Andi's and Levi's ears. "Let me go, or I'll tell Mama you're spying on—"

Andi clapped a frantic hand over the little girl's mouth, but it was too late.

"What is going on up there?" Mother strolled into the foyer and looked up at the landing. Behind her, Katherine and Mr. Powers waited. "Andrea, I asked you a question. Please come down."

Uh-oh. Being caught eavesdropping was not how Andi wanted to finish her day. She threw a disgusted look at Betsy and slowly made her way down the stairs. The two younger children followed in silence.

When all three stood before her, Mother nodded. "I'm waiting."

"I'm sorry for eavesdropping, Mother," Andi apologized. "We wanted to hear what Mr. Powers and Kate were talking about, and what would happen to Levi."

"I see. All right, then. You might as well hear. Katherine?"

Katherine stepped forward and looked sorrowfully at her son. "What you did was wrong, Levi, very wrong. The marbles were returned, but the injury you caused Jacob cannot be overlooked. I assured Mr. Powers that you will be punished with the switch for hurting his son."

Levi made a sound like a frightened puppy and clutched Andi's sleeve.

Andi didn't shake him off like she normally would have. Instead, her heart hurt for her pesky nephew. She knew what it was like to be worried about a whipping. Mr. Foster had been ready to give her one two months ago—until Chad walked in and rescued her.

Chad would not be rescuing Levi. But maybe there was something Andi could do—if she was brave enough. *Maybe.*

Katherine's blue eyes filled with tears at her son's hopeless expression. "Oh, Levi! How could you cause me such sorrow?" She bowed her head. Her thin shoulders shook with quiet sobs.

Levi found his voice. "Don't cry, Mama. It wasn't my fault. Honest."

"Levi Joseph," Katherine warned between sobs, "don't add lying to your—"

"Levi's right," Andi said.

Everyone turned to her in surprise.

"How's that, young lady?" Mr. Powers folded his arms across his chest and silently demanded an explanation.

Andi swallowed. As much as she disliked Levi, it didn't seem right that he should be punished so severely his first day of school. "It's *my* fault."

Levi gawked at her. Katherine's mouth fell open.

"It was Levi's first day of school," Andi explained. "I should have watched out for him, showed him around, and told him the rules. If I'd been with him, he would not have stolen Jacob's marbles. That would have kept him out of the fight. I'll watch him better from now on, if you'll let him off from getting switched."

She straightened her shoulders and turned to Mr. Powers. "If you insist on punishing someone, you can ask Justin to . . . to . . ." She paused. "Well, you can ask him to switch *me.*"

Mother stared at Andi as if seeing her for the first time. Her face showed her surprise.

"I see." Mr. Powers rubbed his cheek, frowned, and took a deep breath. "A very interesting offer, young lady. Are you just saying words, or do you mean it?"

"I mean it. I know Levi's a lot of trouble, but it was his first day among strangers."

Mr. Powers and Andi locked gazes for a full minute. Then he sighed. "Very well. I'll leave this matter in Justin's hands, so long as *that boy*"—he pointed his finger at Levi—"stays far away from my son. Is that understood?"

"Yes, sir," Andi agreed.

Mr. Powers nodded curtly. "You've got yourself quite a job." He turned on his heel and headed for the front door. Opening it, he paused. "Good day, Mrs. Carter, Mrs. Swanson. Thank you for your time."

The door closed. Katherine sank into a nearby chair and let her tears flow once more.

"Aw, Mama," Levi burst out, "don't start crying again. I'll leave that ol' Jacob Powers alone."

"Indeed you will, young man," Mother broke in. "But for now, you will march out to the woodpile and bring in a full load of wood for the box in the kitchen. Later, when your Uncle Mitch comes in from the range, you'll do whatever chores he assigns you, without a word of complaint."

Levi gaped at his grandmother. "But . . ." His voice trailed off at the expression on her face. He looked at Katherine. "Mama?"

Katherine shook her head and didn't speak.

"March," Mother ordered.

Levi took off running toward the kitchen.

Andi hid a pleased smile behind her hand. So far, Mother had been unusually patient and loving toward Levi. She had put up with his sassy mouth and stomping feet without a word.

Andi wouldn't dare talk to her mother the way Levi talked to Katherine. This sudden change of attitude in his grandmother seemed to frighten Levi, and Andi was glad. Somebody had to make Levi mind, and Katherine didn't appear up to the task.

"Forgive me for interfering, Katherine," Mother said, "but I'm afraid I can no longer allow Levi to misbehave. I tried to give him time to settle in, but his attitude is affecting the entire household."

Katherine sighed. "You needn't apologize, Mother. I'm embarrassed to admit how dreadful Levi behaves. Honestly, I never noticed, not until we arrived here. I had so many things on my mind—like surviving and getting away from Troy—that raising my children was set aside."

"I understand, dear." Mother turned to Andi. "Andrea, you certainly silenced Mr. Powers with your surprising offer. I'm proud of you."

Andi bit her lip. It felt good at the time to help Levi out of a tight spot, but she didn't feel very good right now. "Is Justin going to . . . ?" She faltered.

Andi couldn't remember a time when anyone but Mother had given her a richly deserved smack on the backside, or even a serious switching. But now? *What have I gotten myself into?* She squirmed.

Mother drew Andi into a warm embrace. "Not if I have anything to say about it. Mr. Powers left the decision in Justin's hands, but I'm sure your brother will agree that the matter is settled."

A load of worry fell from Andi's shoulders. She hugged Mother.

Katherine stood up. "Andi, I'd like to speak with you. Would you join me in the library?"

Andi hesitated.

"Please?"

Up until now, she'd avoided spending time alone with Katherine. Three weeks had not yet melted all the resentment she still harbored against her sister's unexpected return. True, Andi had begun to accept and even feel a little warmth toward the children, especially

Betsy, but she wasn't ready to welcome Katherine with open arms. Not yet.

She drew away from her mother's arms and nodded at Katherine. "I guess so."

Tentatively, Katherine put an arm around Andi's shoulder and led her down the hall and into the library. She closed the doors and sat down on the wide settee. "Would you sit beside me?"

Andi sat stiffly, prepared for the worst.

"I want to thank you for putting up with us these past few weeks," Katherine said. "I know you resent my being here."

Andi winced as she heard her sister speak the truth aloud. She opened her mouth, but Katherine shook her head and kept talking.

"Mother spends a lot of time with me and the children, and I know it bothers you. I've seen the hurt in your eyes when the boys and I are laughing over old times, times you can't share."

Andi ducked her head. Yes, it hurt. A lot.

"Melinda remembers me and enjoys having a big sister around again," Katherine went on. "But you already have a big sister, and I'm nothing more than a stranger who has turned your family head over heels. I'm sorry, Andi. I truly didn't mean to cause you so much heartache with my return. I would leave if—"

Andi leaped to her feet. "You mustn't leave! It would break Mother's heart. She'd cry, and I couldn't stand that. Besides, Justin would skin me alive if you left on my account. Please don't go."

Katherine smiled and drew Andi back to her side. "I'm not leaving yet. I just wanted you to know how grateful I am for your patience."

Andi flushed, suddenly ashamed. She hadn't been patient because she wanted to be, only because Justin had insisted and she'd promised Mother that she'd try.

"I know my children aren't the best behaved kids in the valley," Katherine was saying. "Levi, especially, has a chip on his shoulder that's begging to be knocked off. I worried that you and he might come to blows those first few days after we arrived."

Andi gave Katherine a tiny smile. "It crossed my mind a couple of times, but Levi's strong for his size, and quick. He would've licked me, just like he did Jacob."

Katherine nodded. "He's had his share of brawls, I'm sorry to say. Yet you stood up for him this afternoon. I can't imagine why. And you've allowed Betsy to tag along behind you most days. I'd like to thank you for that. It's real nice of you. She talks about you constantly. 'Andi showed me the kittens in the hayloft.' 'Andi let me brush Taffy.' 'When Andi gets home from school, we'll go riding.'"

She chuckled. "You get the idea. Betsy needs someone like you to pay attention to her, someone she can look up to. Perhaps you haven't done it joyfully, but she hasn't noticed."

Andi squirmed as the truth stung her conscience. Katherine was right. Most of the time she *hadn't* done it joyfully. She'd been kind to Betsy and Hannah partly because of Justin's scolding and partly because she didn't want to worry her mother.

Please, God, she prayed silently, *forgive me for my bad attitude. I'm sorry. Help me love my sister and her children. They've had a hard life, and I've been too selfish to care.*

When Andi raised her head, she smiled at Katherine. A real smile. She squeezed her sister's hand. "When you first came, I was so angry. Angry that nobody told me about you, angry that people were gossiping about our family. I didn't want anyone saying I looked like you, because I was embarrassed that you're my sister."

"I don't blame you," Katherine said with a sigh. "I've been an embarrassment to my family more than once over the years."

"But now," Andi said. "I . . . well . . . I guess I don't mind so much that you're here. I'm getting used to you. In fact," she admitted, "if you stay much longer, I might even learn to love you."

With a cry of joy, Katherine pulled Andi into her arms. For once, Andi didn't try to get away. She let her sister hug her. "You don't know how much your words mean to me," Katherine whispered.

She sat up and brushed away her tears. "I feel much better about leaving the children here while I'm gone."

"What do you mean? You're not leaving."

"I'm going to San Francisco for a couple of weeks."

"Why?"

"Aunt Rebecca has invited us to stay with her for as long as we like."

"I thought you were staying here. Justin told me you could stay as long as you wanted."

"Only until I get settled in the city," Katherine said.

"You can't leave. Mother will cry."

"Mother knows about my plans," Katherine said. "She knows I'm not suited for ranch life. I never have been. It's enough to know that I'm welcome for a visit now and again. I'd like to make arrangements for some kind of employment in the city, before I take the children."

"Are you going by yourself?"

"I'd planned to, but if you don't mind, I'd like to invite Mother along."

Andi frowned, puzzled. "Why would I mind?"

"I don't want to hurt you again by taking Mother away from you for two weeks." She grasped Andi's hands and grinned. "I just thought of a splendid idea. Why don't you come along? It could be the three of us."

Andi sucked in her breath. San Francisco? Aunt Rebecca? She shook her head. "You're not suited for ranch life, and I'm not suited for city life. I'd rather stay here and help out with the kids."

She stood up and gave her sister's hand a tug. "Come on, Kate. Let's find Mother. I want to see the look on her face when you invite her to go to San Francisco."

Chapter Eleven

AN EMPTY HOUSE

The house felt huge and empty with her mother gone.

"Of course, it really isn't empty," Andi kept telling herself. "Far from it."

Luisa and Nila still bustled about, performing their usual tasks. Andi's brothers were in and out. Katherine's children had made themselves at home, and the clamor of their crashing feet and high-pitched squeals kept everything in an uproar.

Yet to Andi, the house was empty without her mother's strong, calming influence and matter-of-fact management. Andi missed her a lot.

Melinda, however, slid effortlessly into the position of mistress of the house. With obvious delight, she oversaw the running of the household, planned the meals, and tried to keep Betsy and Hannah corralled—not an easy task.

More than once, Andi came home from school to find her sister locked in a battle of wills with Betsy. It was clear which aunt the little girl preferred. Her tears and temper tantrums ceased the moment Andi arrived home. Unfortunately, this meant Andi found herself with a tagalong for the rest of the afternoon and evening.

During this time, the weather changed for the worse. Summer's dust turned into ankle-deep mud when it rained, which it did for a solid week. The streets of Fresno were dotted with puddles and thick with sloppy mire.

Never had the town seen so much rain in November. The old-timers gossiped. The ladies complained. Winter rains didn't usually appear until after the holidays. Why an early showing this year?

"This term feels like it's never going to end." Andi picked her way with Levi across muddy Tulare Street to Justin's office for a ride home after school. They'd already crossed four other streets, and their shoes were caked with mud.

Andi pulled her cloak tighter around herself and glanced up. Dark clouds scudded across the sky. It looked as if it might rain again any minute. When it did, she would get soaked. "Hurry up, Levi, before we get caught in a downpour."

Levi leaped onto the boardwalk in front of Justin's office. "I like this weather."

"Why, for goodness' sake?" Andi preferred sunny fall days and cool, crisp nights.

"Cuz it makes good mud balls." Levi reached down and scooped up a glob of the sticky stuff from the street with his bare hands. "Watch."

Andi watched Levi form a small ball. His hands oozed with mud. Dirty water seeped between his fingers and dripped onto his britches. "What are you going to do with it?" she asked. "Tim won't let you in Justin's office all muddy like that."

"You'll see." He patted his mud ball and hid it behind his back. Then he leaned against a lamppost near Andi and waited.

Andi gave him a puzzled look and opened her mouth to speak.

"Shh!" Levi put a grubby finger in front of his lips. Then he settled back to wait some more. Several minutes later, he straightened up, took aim, and hurled the ball of mud across the street.

Splat!

The mud ball splattered against the neck of a nicely dressed gentleman just leaving the land office. With a startled cry, he peered behind his shoulder, slapped wildly at his plastered neck, and whirled around.

It was Matthew Powers, Jacob's father.

"Levi!" Andi whispered in a choked voice. She looked around. Levi had disappeared.

She backed against the door to Justin's office and held her breath. Mr. Powers turned a wary glance up and down Tulare Street. His face was bright red. He looked ready to burst.

What if he crosses the street and asks me if I saw who did it? Fearing he might, Andi fumbled for the doorknob and gave it a hasty turn. She hurried into the office and slammed the door shut. Without a word to Justin's clerk, she crossed the room, sat down in a chair, and stared at the floor.

"Well?" Tim demanded from his desk.

"I'm waiting for Justin. It's cold outside."

Tim grunted and returned to his work.

A few minutes later, the door opened and in walked Levi. His hands and face were clean, and most of the mud had been scraped from his britches. Only a few dark streaks remained. His eyes sparkled. He took a seat beside Andi, folded his hands in his lap, and looked at her.

Andi shot a quick glance at Tim then leaned close to Levi's ear. "Are you *loco*? Matthew Powers, of all people."

"Serves him right for sticking his nose in and making my mother cry." He gave Andi a warm, friendly grin, the first real smile she'd ever received from him. "I did it for you too. He wanted to see you thrashed, sure as shootin'."

Andi didn't know how to respond to Levi's words. On the one hand, he'd plastered an innocent bystander with a mud ball and should be scolded. On the other hand, he'd just offered Andi the one thing she never thought she'd receive from him—friendship.

She chose the latter.

"Looks like another storm's rolling in." Chad tossed his hat aside and crossed the library, where the rest of the family had gathered to read the paper or play games. With a teasing scowl, he bent over the checkerboard and pronounced judgment. "Little sister, you are in a heap of trouble. One wrong move and Levi will jump a good number of your pieces."

Andi lifted a red checker.

Chad cringed. "Not that one."

"Uncle Chad! No fair!" Levi protested. "You can't help her."

"Don't worry, Levi," Andi said. "I never pay Chad any mind when it comes to checkers. I beat him most every time." She smiled smugly at her brother.

Chad shrugged and sank into an overstuffed chair by the fire. He picked up the *Expositor* and began reading, a sure sign he had no idea how the checkers game would end.

"Finish your move," Levi growled.

Andi plunked her checker down and sat back to wait. Levi jumped her piece with a quiet laugh. Just as she'd hoped, Levi had stumbled into her trap.

Like lightning, Andi moved in for the kill. She jumped Levi's remaining pieces, collected them, and tossed them into the box. "I win."

Levi folded his arms across his chest and sulked. "You *always* win."

"Not always. Just most of the time. Another game?"

"Not me." He stood up and wandered over to watch Mitch clean a rifle.

Andi gathered up the rest of the checkers, relieved at Levi's mellow reaction to losing the game. The first time he'd lost—less than a month ago—he'd overturned the board into Andi's lap, shoved her to the floor, and stormed away, swearing.

Over the past few weeks, however, a subtle change had come over him. He no longer cussed, and his bad moods came further and further apart. Since the day Andi had offered to take his whipping, he hadn't once called her "auntie." She was actually beginning to enjoy spending time with her nephew.

She glanced over to see Levi's brown head bent close to Mitch's blond one. They appeared to be in a deep discussion about rifles. Levi pointed to something and laughed. Mitch reached out and tousled the boy's hair.

Poor Levi, Andi realized suddenly. *He hasn't got a father. He hasn't any big brothers, either. No wonder Mitch spends so much time with him.*

"Andi." Justin's voice pulled her from her musing. "The clock struck nine. You and the younger ones better be getting to bed."

Andi pulled herself from her comfortable spot near the checkerboard and yawned. At the same time, Melinda gathered up a sleeping Hannah and started for the stairs.

"Want me to take Betsy?" Andi offered.

Melinda nodded gratefully.

"I'll see Levi to bed in a minute," Mitch called from across the room as a sleepy Betsy slid from the settee and took Andi's hand.

Before long, the little girl was settled in the room she shared with Hannah. Andi stumbled wearily to her own room and curled up under the bed coverings. Helping with Hannah was so exhausting, she didn't mind being sent to bed with the children.

A low rumble woke Andi from a sound sleep. She didn't know how late it was, but her room was pitch black. Suddenly, a pale light flashed through the French doors leading to the balcony. Another distant rumble followed.

Andi pulled the covers over her head. A thunderstorm! She knew it was far away, up in the hills, but that knowledge couldn't chase away her fear. When she was little, she had often rushed to her parents' room and thrown herself into their bed during a thunderstorm.

Well, her mother wasn't here now, and she doubted anyone else would appreciate a midnight visitor. She clapped her hands over her ears as the thunder came closer.

Another loud crash yanked Andi from beneath her covers. She sat up and peered through the gloom. Her bedroom door hung open. A flash of lightning revealed Betsy trembling and crying in the doorway.

Andi held out her arms. A clap of thunder propelled Betsy into action. She flew across the room and sailed into Andi's bed. Together, the two girls buried themselves under the covers and waited for the storm to pass.

"I'm scared," Betsy whimpered as another roll of thunder sounded.

"It's a long ways off," Andi assured Betsy. And herself. "It won't come here."

"What if it does?" Betsy asked in a quivering voice. "Back home, the thunder made me scream. It shook the whole house. Once, lightning came down the chimney." She started crying in earnest.

Andi wanted to cry too. She hated thunderstorms. But she had to be brave for Betsy's sake. "Well then"—she kept her voice calm and reassuring—"let's pretend we're hiding in a deep cave under the mountains. The thunder and lightning can't get us there. We'll be two little black bears hibernating for the winter. We'll cuddle up together and fall asleep in our warm cave, where the storm can't come. When we wake up, it'll be spring."

Betsy stopped crying. Clearly, the game of being a little black bear cub interested her. "What're our names?" Her voice no longer trembled.

Slowly, Andi wove an exciting tale of two mischievous bear cubs named Cuffy and Jasper. By the time the rumbling faded and the storm moved deeper into the mountains, Betsy was sound asleep, no doubt dreaming of baby bears and warm caves.

Andi folded back the quilt and breathed in some fresh air. Against the French doors of her balcony, she heard the pattering of raindrops. With a weary sigh, she curled up next to Betsy, pulled the covers around her shoulders, and fell asleep to the music of rain against glass.

Chapter Twelve

A VISIT FROM TJ

"W hen is Mother coming home?" Andi asked at breakfast the next morning. She speared a slab of ham and slid it onto her plate. "It's been weeks."

"Honestly, Andi," Melinda said. "She's only been gone six days. I expect they'll be home in another week."

"Another week?" Andi sighed. "It shouldn't take that long to find a position and visit Aunt Rebecca. Mother's got to be home for Thanksgiving, and that's next Thursday." She studied her slice of ham. "You and Nila cook ham fine, but only Mother knows how to do the turkey right."

"She'll be here in time," Melinda assured her. "Don't you like the way I'm running the house?"

"Oh, sure." Andi rearranged the eggs on her plate. "You're doing a terrific job. I just miss Mother at night. Especially last night."

Justin chuckled. "That doesn't surprise me, knowing your fondness for thunderstorms."

"Me an' Andi *hate* thunderstorms," Betsy piped up. "We slept in a deep, dark cave, where the thunder couldn't get us."

"That's nice." Justin smiled at the little girl. He dropped his napkin onto the table and stood up. "I see Chad and Mitch have already left. Is Levi with them?"

Andi nodded. "He asked me early this morning to go riding with him, but it's such a dreary day that I didn't want to go. Mitch said Levi could follow the hands around and watch them repair fences."

"Sounds exciting," Justin said, in a voice that meant the opposite. "I've got some paperwork to take care of this morning, so I'll be in the library." He smiled at Melinda. "Delicious breakfast, honey. Give my compliments to the cook."

Melinda beamed. "Nila was busy with the churning, so I did the cooking this morning."

"I thought so." He left the dining room, whistling.

Two hours later, Andi wished she'd taken Levi up on his offer to go riding. There was absolutely nothing of interest going on in the yard. She and Betsy had brushed and groomed Taffy until she shone.

Andi had done all her Saturday chores: fed and watered the stabled horses, collected the eggs with Betsy's help, and taken the newly churned butter to the springhouse. Still, the morning threatened to drag on for hours.

She was in the corral, showing Betsy how to put a bridle on a small, chocolate-colored pony, when a cheerful voice called out a greeting.

Andi whirled and saw TJ Silver making his way across the yard. "TJ! Howdy." She was delighted to see him. "Are you working for us? Did Sid give you a job? Whatcha been doing?"

TJ grinned through his beard. He held up a hand and called out, "Hold on. One question at a time, please."

Andi helped Betsy into the pony's saddle and handed her the reins. "Here you go. Don't be afraid. Coco can't get out. You can ride him around and around as much as you like."

Betsy slammed her heels into the pony's flank and shouted, but the little animal merely turned his head and looked at her. Then he carefully picked up his hooves and plodded slowly around the inside of the corral. Betsy squealed her delight.

TJ joined Andi at the fence. "That little pony sure doesn't let much excite him."

"Nope. He's old and set in his ways. No matter how hard Betsy kicks him, he won't break into anything faster than a trot."

"A good first pony," TJ said.

"He was mine." Andi climbed over the corral fence and jumped to the ground. "And Melinda's, and Mitch's." She grinned. "All of us had Coco for our first pony. Justin named him."

TJ nodded toward Betsy. "Is she your little sister?"

"No, she's Levi's sister. You remember Levi?"

"The spunky young fella who chased after you up by the creek?" When Andi nodded, TJ chuckled. "Didn't get a chance to meet him, I'm afraid." He looked around. "Where is he this morning?"

"With Chad and Mitch. I think they're checking fences, or pretending to for Levi's sake. He likes to play cowhand every chance he gets."

TJ rested his arms across the top rail of the fence and watched Betsy circle the corral. "Cute kid," he remarked. "Will your niece and nephew be staying with you long?"

Andi boosted herself to the top of the fence. "Only until my sister finds work in San Francisco. That's where she and my mother have been for the past week. Kate's looking for work. She doesn't like ranches. She wants to live in the city."

TJ glanced around with approval in his eyes. "This is a fine ranch, Andi. Your sister must be *loco* not to want to stay here."

Andi couldn't have agreed more. Who wouldn't want to live in wide-open spaces with sun, fresh air, sweet hay, and horses? It warmed her heart to hear that TJ felt the same way. "Do you like working for my brothers?" she asked.

"Haven't seen 'em much," TJ confessed. "But Sid's a good foreman. The work's hard, but the pay's good, and the Circle C has the best grub this side of the Sierras." He grinned. "A fella can't ask for more than that."

"What about family? You got any?" Andi knew she was breaking an unspoken rule by asking a hired hand about his past, but she couldn't help it. She'd rescued him from certain death and felt she had the right to know a little bit about him.

It was clear TJ didn't agree. His eyes narrowed at the question, and he lost his smile. "I had a family . . . once." He turned a dark look on Andi. "Don't ask me about them again."

Andi's mouth fell open. She was about to stutter an apology for prying, when Levi's shrill voice split the air.

"Andi! We got a letter from Mama!" He raced Patches up to Andi and yanked the pony to a stop, waving the letter above his head. Ignoring TJ, he slid from the paint horse and presented the cream-colored envelope to Andi. "Mitch took me to town to fetch the mail. We opened it, and Mama and Grandmother are coming home day after tomorrow."

His huge grin and sparkling eyes told Andi how much he missed his mother.

"Yippee!" Andi shouted her joy. She missed *her* mother too.

"It also says Aunt Rebecca won't hear of Mama taking some low, common job," Levi prattled on. "She wants us to live with her and keep her company. She's gonna send me and Betsy to school and buy all of us new clothes and teach us to be fine, fancy folks." He wrinkled his brow. "Is she rich, Andi?"

"Very rich." Andi glanced at the envelope in her hand. "The letter said all that?"

"Yep. And there's lots more, but Mama said she'd explain when she gets back." He grinned. "I can't wait!"

"I thought you liked living on the ranch," Andi said quietly. Now that it looked like Katherine and the kids were leaving, Andi wasn't sure she wanted them to go.

Levi's face fell. "I do like it here, but I miss the adventure of the city. There's always something exciting happening there." Then he brightened. "Just cuz I leave doesn't mean I can't come back for a visit."

He snatched the envelope out of Andi's hand. "Mama says we're leaving the day after Thanksgiving. I guess that means no more riding or racing. I'm sorta sorry about that."

Andi jumped down from the fence and put an arm around Levi's shoulder. "Tell you what. Maybe we can talk Justin into letting us go riding tomorrow after church, if the weather isn't too bad."

Levi nodded. "I gotta beat you at least once before I go." He ducked under Andi's arm, grabbed the reins of his paint horse, and headed for the barn. "I'm going up to the house to tell Justin and Melinda that Mama's coming home. See ya later."

"Sure. See ya." With Levi gone, Andi turned her attention back to Betsy. The little girl was riding around the corral, paying no attention to the conversation. She kicked Coco and hummed a little tune. Andi waved to her and turned to speak to TJ.

He was gone.

Chapter Thirteen

AN AFTERNOON RIDE

"Uncle Justin, can me and Andi go riding after dinner?" Levi asked on the way home from church the next day. "I'm not used to sitting still so long, not even in school. It feels like a million spiders are crawling around inside my belly."

"You want to come up and drive the team?" Justin asked.

"Sure!" Levi scrambled over the back of the seat and took his place between Justin and Melinda. "But I still want to go riding," he said as he took the reins.

"Reverend Harris did seem to go on and on today," Melinda agreed with a sigh. "I'm worn out from trying to keep Hannah still."

From the back seat, Andi joined the plea. "Please, Justin? It might be the last chance Levi gets to ride around the ranch for a long, long time."

Justin chuckled. "All right, all right. You may go, so long as the weather holds."

Cheers greeted Justin's permission. The rest of the ride home passed quickly. They pulled into the yard, and Justin brought the matched pair of bay horses to a stop. He climbed down and came around to the other side of the carriage, where he reached up and took Hannah from Melinda. To the child's shrieks of delight, he swung her high in the air then set her gently on her feet.

"Me too!" Betsy climbed over Andi to get to her uncle.

When Betsy was safely on the ground, Justin helped his sisters from the carriage. Levi leaped out of the rig and took off running toward the house. "Come on," he shouted. "I'm hungry."

After a dinner of fried chicken, mashed potatoes and gravy, biscuits, and apple cobbler, Andi felt too full to ride. She stepped out of the house and glanced toward the mountains. A stiff breeze was blowing, driving thick gray clouds up against the foothills.

She shivered. When would the sunny November days Andi was used to return?

The door banged and Levi joined Andi on the porch. "Ready to go for a ride?"

"It looks like it's going to rain soon," Andi said. "There's nothing worse than riding in the rain. Let's play checkers instead."

Levi pointed to a break in the clouds. A sliver of sunlight touched the hills. "It's sunny where we're going, Andi. Please? Justin said we could." He looked at her with pleading eyes. "Just a short ride?"

"Oh, all right," Andi gave in. Then she grinned. "You're getting mighty good at sweet-talking. All those city girls will be falling at your feet in no time."

Levi thrust Andi's hand aside. "Don't talk like a sissy girl!" He stomped off toward the barn, his high spirits clearly dampened.

Andi kicked herself mentally. Levi was speaking nicely to her, and she'd teased him. She ran up behind him and laid an apologetic hand on his shoulder. "I'm sorry. I was just kidding. Don't be sore."

Levi turned around and eyed Andi. Then he jerked his chin toward the barn. "Let's ride."

When Betsy and Hannah discovered they were being left behind, they put up such a fuss that Andi gave in. "Let's see what Justin says."

All smiles, they tagged along after Andi to find Justin. "I'll look after them," she promised. "If it starts to rain even one drop, I'll bring everybody home."

Justin glanced at the sky. He looked ready to change his mind about the afternoon ride.

"It's breaking up over the foothills," Andi argued. "We won't be gone long. Just up to my special spot, throw some rocks in the water, and maybe challenge Levi to a horserace."

Levi's smile stretched from ear to ear.

"All right," Justin agreed. "It does look like the sun might win, after all. But don't be gone long. Two hours should be plenty of time for what you want to do." His look turned serious. "Be back on time, or I'll send the entire ranch after you. You know what will happen then."

Oh, yes. Andi knew. It was no fun to be dragged home like a stray calf just because she lost track of the time. "I don't want Chad mad at me for disturbing everybody's day off. We'll be back with time to spare"—she grinned—"especially if you let me borrow your watch."

Justin handed over his pocket watch, which Andi stuffed into the pocket of her split skirt. She and Levi saddled their horses and led them out of the barn. By now, the sun had cleared a good portion of clouds from the sky. It shone down warm and friendly. At last!

Levi tossed his heavy jacket aside. "I sure don't need this."

"You might be sorry," Andi warned, settling herself on Taffy.

Levi ignored her and mounted Patches.

Justin lifted Betsy into Coco's saddle and handed Levi the lead rope. "I know you're a big girl, Betsy, but today Levi will lead Coco, all right?"

Betsy nodded and gripped the saddle horn.

Justin plopped Hannah down in front of Andi, "I want you to remember that these children are your responsibility. You're in charge."

"Sure, Justin." She threw a delighted grin in Levi's direction.

Justin frowned. "I'm serious. Levi may act like he can take care of himself, but you know the ranch. Use your head to keep everybody out of trouble, all right?"

"Does that mean I have to mind her?" Levi grumbled from the paint horse's back.

Justin gave Levi a firm look. "That's exactly what it means, young man. Do you think you can do that?"

"I reckon." He shrugged. "If it's the only way I get to ride today."

"It is," Justin replied. "Now go on and have a good time. I'll see you later."

Andi nudged Taffy. The mare took off at a gentle trot.

Hannah squealed. She raised her hand and waved. "Bye, Uncle Justin!" she shouted. "Bye!"

They started out slowly, mostly to give Betsy and her small pony a chance to keep up. Levi brought Patches alongside Taffy and yanked on Coco's lead line.

"It's a long way up to the creek," Andi told him. "Keep a tight hold on that pony. It's the only way we'll get him to go faster than a walk."

Hannah looked perfectly content. Under one arm, she clutched her doll, Tessie. She sucked her thumb and leaned back into the warmth of Andi's body. Whenever she saw Betsy and Levi draw near, she pulled out her thumb and yelled, "See me! I'm riding. I'm riding."

When they came to a flat place, Andi took the lead rope from Levi and allowed him to run Patches at a full gallop. She watched with admiration. Levi could really ride. He stood up in his stirrups and shouted his usual Indian war whoop, then circled around and pretended to knock Andi off her horse. The little girls screamed their laughter.

Levi took a turn holding Hannah and the lead rope, so Andi could enjoy the opportunity to gallop Taffy through the dry, golden grass.

Andi reined in beside him. "What about our race? There's a long, level stretch not too far from where we're headed that makes a terrific racetrack. We could leave Betsy and Hannah under a tree for a few minutes. Want to?"

"You bet! Here." Levi handed Andi the lead rope and jabbed Patches in the sides. He took off up a hill.

Andi followed, pulling on Coco's lead line. The pony snorted but broke into a bouncy trot. Betsy squealed. "Faster, Coco!"

"Sorry, Betsy," Andi said with a laugh. "Coco's short legs won't let him go much faster." She kept the pony at a fast trot and let Hannah hold Taffy's reins with her.

Straight ahead, Andi's favorite spot on the entire ranch opened up. The Sierra Nevada range rose in the distance. Clouds were gathering again, covering the peaks like a thick, fluffy quilt. To the right, the creek gurgled. No longer a muddy trickle, the recent rains had swelled the stream nearly to its banks. Oak trees dotted the hills.

Andi sighed. Even in late November, this place was beautiful. She reined Taffy to a stop under an old oak tree and slid from the saddle. When she lifted Hannah to the ground, the little girl started running alongside the creek.

"Stay away from the creek," Andi warned. "It's cold and deep right now."

Hannah obediently skipped back a few steps. Betsy joined her. They picked up rocks and began tossing them into the water as if it were the grandest game in the world.

Levi joined Andi and put his hands on his hips. "So, are we gonna race or what?"

"Yes!"

Andi called to the girls. "Come over here and sit down a minute. Levi and I are going to race. You get to decide who wins."

The girls hurried over and plopped themselves down under the tree. "I'll say *go*," Betsy said. She reached out and grasped her little sister's hand. "And I'll make sure Hannah doesn't run off and fall in the creek."

"Good girl," Andi praised her. "We'll only be a few minutes." She swung into her saddle and pointed to a huge, ancient oak a couple hundred yards away. "We race to the tree, go around it, then back to this spot. That way Betsy can see who passes the finish line first. Fair?"

Levi nodded. "Fair enough." He hunkered down in the saddle and gripped the reins.

Andi did the same. "Ready, Betsy?"

Betsy nodded. "Ready—*go!*"

The two horses took off.

Andi was more experienced at racing and had the better horse. However, Patches looked determined to give the mare a run for her money. They reached the oak. Andi rounded it slightly ahead of Levi. Levi caught up as they galloped the last fifty yards. They raced neck and neck past the tree where they'd left the little girls.

Levi shrieked his delight. "Did I win?"

"I don't know. It sure was close." Andi met Levi as he reined Patches to a stop. "I think it was a tie. Want to race again?"

"You bet! I'm sure Patches will win by a length this time, now that he knows the lay of the land."

Andi laughed. "Let's check with the girls first. Betsy's supposed to be judging this race. Maybe you won, after all."

She turned Taffy around and loped back to the tree. "Betsy, who won the—?"

Andi yanked Taffy to a stop and stared at the empty spot under the tree.

Betsy and Hannah were gone.

Chapter Fourteen

A DANGEROUS DISCOVERY

L evi pulled up beside Andi and stammered, "They're g-gone."
"I can see that!" Andi snapped. She tried to breathe. It felt as
if a giant fist were squeezing the air from her lungs. She slid from
Taffy's back and hit the ground with a *thud*. Then she raced to the
creek. "Betsy! Hannah!" she screamed.

There was no answer.

Oh, God, where are they? Andi stood on the bank, her gaze riv-
eted on the roiling, swirling water. A sob caught in her throat. She
shouldn't have left the girls alone, not even for a minute. Justin had
trusted her to look after them.

Please don't let them be in the creek! she prayed silently.

Levi ran up and grabbed her arm. "What are we gonna do? We
can't just stand here. We gotta find 'em. What if they fell in the—"

"Shut up and let me think!" Fear made her words harsh. She
shook Levi off and tried to come up with a plan. But she couldn't
think. She could only stare numbly at the muddy water sloshing over
her boot tops. Her stomach felt tied in knots.

"They're right here, safe and sound," a voice called over the noisy
creek.

Andi spun around.

A tall, handsome man was leading Betsy and Hannah toward her.

"I didn't want these two little ones to fall in the creek," he said with a friendly grin, "so I took 'em for a walk."

Andi rushed over and gathered the girls in her arms. Hannah was crying. Betsy looked close to tears. "Don't cry. You're all right." She buried her face in their hair and hugged them tight. Never had she been so frightened. "Thank You, God." Happy tears stung her eyes.

She took a deep breath, blinked away her tears, and glanced up. "You scared me half to death, mister. Didn't you see Levi and me racing? We were in plain sight." She straightened up and faced him. "I mean . . . well . . . it's not that I'm ungrateful, but the girls were perfectly safe where we left them. You needn't—"

She broke off. The man looked strangely familiar. She frowned. "Do I know you?"

"It's me, Andi." He spread his arms and turned a full circle. "TJ. I used my first week's pay to buy some new clothes, get a shave, and clean up. What do you think?"

Andi wasn't ready to forgive TJ for scaring her so badly. "I think it was downright mean of you to take the girls for a walk. Why didn't you wait with them under the tree?"

TJ shrugged. "I reckon I should have, but—"

"Let's go." Levi came up beside Andi and tugged on her hand. "Right now."

"We just got here." Andi peeled his fingers away. "The girls are safe. TJ was with them. He's the fella I told you about. The one we found up here a few weeks ago. He works for us now."

Levi shook his head. "I want to go home. Now."

TJ crossed his arms over his chest. "What's the matter, boy? There's no call to go running off. Haven't seen you for quite a spell. How are you?" When Levi didn't answer, TJ lowered his arms to his sides and took a step forward. "Answer me."

"I'm f-fine, Pa," Levi stuttered, stepping back. He yanked on Andi's sleeve. "Please, Andi. Let's go home."

Andi didn't move. She stood frozen, staring at TJ and trying to make sense of what Levi had just said. *Pa? That can't be right.* "What's going on? Why did Levi call you his pa?"

"Because that's who I am."

Andi's heart plunged clear to her toes. "You said your name was TJ Silver."

He shrugged. "TJ, Troy. What's the difference?" He chuckled. "The look on your face is precious, Andi. Don't you realize a name is the easiest thing in the world to change?"

Betsy sniffled, but Andi shushed her.

"The rest was a bit more difficult," TJ was saying. "The hair, my beard. But the run-in with those ruffians worked to my advantage. I could have done without the knifing, though." His smile grew wider at Andi's astonishment.

"Why?" She drew the two little girls closer. "Why didn't you tell me your real name?"

"And give myself away?" TJ shook his head. "Not a chance. The minute I opened my eyes, I knew I was on the Circle C. You look enough like my Katie to be her twin sister. Even if she wasn't on the ranch yet, I knew she'd show up eventually. I wanted to lay low 'til I was ready."

"Ready for what?" Andi already knew the answer.

"Don't pretend you don't know. I've come for my family. Thanks to your willingness to bring me supplies and keep my presence a secret, I was able to rest and regain my strength."

Andi groaned.

"When I saw Levi at the creek, I knew Katie was here," TJ went on. "I disguised myself the best I could and tried to stay clear of the kids. I used the job you helped me find as an excuse to stick around the ranch. I needed to figure out the best way to get my wife and kids back."

He walked over and clapped a hand on Levi's shoulder. "I've got plans for us, boy. Big plans. In a few days your mother will meet us, and we can be a family again."

"What if she doesn't want to?" Andi lifted Hannah into her arms. Betsy hung onto Andi's riding skirt and stared at her father.

TJ's look turned dark. "She doesn't have a choice. I don't take kindly to my wife running off with my kids. It's taken me a long time to track her down. When I finally guessed she was crawling back to her family, I had a good laugh. She must have been desperate if she humbled herself enough to beg your forgiveness."

His lips drew into a sneer. "Wish I could have seen her—the once-proud Katherine Carter—pleading for a place to stay."

Andi erupted into fury. "We should have left you in the creek!"

TJ laughed. "True enough, but you wouldn't have done it. You have a kind heart, and you're entirely too trusting. Your friends had the right of it the day you found me. You should have listened to them and been a little more suspicious."

He shrugged. "Anyway, I want to thank you for delivering my children to me." He gave her a mocking bow.

Andi felt dizzy with horror. *What have I done?* She looked at Levi. "I'm sorry, Levi. I didn't know."

"It's not your fault," Levi said bitterly. "You got fooled. Pa's real good at it. He makes his living swindling folks. You didn't stand a chance."

"If only I hadn't tried to keep you away from the creek that day." Andi drew a long, shaky breath. "You would have—"

"Yep." Levi nodded. "I would've recognized him—beard or no beard—if you'd given me half a chance. But you were in such an all-fired hurry to send me back to the ranch. Now it's—"

"Enough chatter. Let's go." TJ yanked Betsy to his side. She burst into tears. "Once Katie learns I have the kids, she'll come running."

"TJ," Andi pleaded, "please. Let's go back to the ranch. When Kate gets home—"

"My name's Troy," he corrected her, "and I'm not going anywhere near your ranch. Your brothers would probably shoot me on sight."

He kept a firm grip on Betsy, who was sobbing in earnest. "Stop that sniveling, Elizabeth. I can't hear to think."

"I want Andi," Betsy wailed. She twisted around and planted a sharp kick on her father's shin.

Troy tossed Betsy aside with a curse.

Sobbing, the little girl sprang to her feet. She ran to Andi and threw her arms around her waist. "I wanna go home. I want Mama."

Andi stroked her hair. "Shh."

Troy motioned to Levi and pointed toward the creek. "My horse is tied up in that clump of scrub oak near the creek. Go get him."

Levi sprang away. A few minutes later, he brought the gelding to a halt in front of his father. His hands and clothes were black with mud, and he was shivering with cold.

Troy snatched the reins from the boy's hands. "What happened?"

Levi cringed. "I t-tripped and f-fell," he explained through chattering teeth.

"Can't you do anything right?"

Troy wrenched Hannah from Andi's arms, mounted his horse, and plopped the little girl down in front of him. Hannah howled.

"What have you Carters done to my kids?" Troy bellowed. "They're nothing but a passel of sniveling, wailing brats. Even Levi looks scared."

Levi flinched at the tone in his father's voice but held his ground. He wrapped his arms around himself for warmth.

"Maybe they're scared of *you*," Andi shot back. She shook with fury and helplessness. This was all her fault. She'd been tricked by TJ's warm and friendly manner, just like he'd probably intended from the start.

She wanted to scream at somebody, and Troy was handy. "You're nothing but a dirty, rotten swindler! I'm glad my sister finally figured it out. Hanging's too good for a low-down skunk like you."

Troy brought his horse alongside Andi and leaned over. With a quick, sharp *smack*, the palm of his hand connected with Andi's face. "Watch your mouth, little sister."

Andi reeled backward, stunned. How dare he hit her! "I'm *not* your little sister, and don't you ever touch me again."

Levi gaped at her, eyes wide.

Blinking back angry tears, Andi stomped over to Levi. "I knew you'd be sorry if you left your jacket home." She pulled off her own warm jacket and helped stuff Levi's soggy arms through the sleeves.

"A real good little Samaritan, aren't you?" Troy sneered. He turned to Levi. "Mount up, son."

"B-but I'm c-cold."

"The sooner we get going, the sooner we'll get to someplace warm and dry. Now, do as I say or you'll feel the back of my hand."

Levi shuffled over to Patches. He pulled himself into the saddle, picked up the reins, and nudged his horse alongside Troy.

"That's more like it," Troy said. "Andi, put Betsy on the pony and bring me the lead rope."

"And if I don't?"

"Well, I've got no reason to be nice to you any longer. If I get off this horse, you'll get more than a slap on the cheek for your sass."

"Do like he says, Andi." Levi sounded scared. "As long as my pa's in a good mood, everything's fine. Don't put him in a bad mood, or else . . ." His voice trailed off when Troy shot him a mean look.

Andi glanced at Betsy, who was trembling with uncertainty. She looked up at Hannah sitting in front of Troy. With her thumb in her mouth, the little girl was whimpering and watching Andi's every move with her round, blue eyes.

"All right." Andi led Coco to Troy and handed him the rope. Then she boosted Betsy onto the back of the pony. "Don't be afraid," she whispered in her ear. "God will take care of us. He'll see to it that you don't fall off Coco."

Andi kissed Betsy's cheek and smiled. "Hang on tight and stick close to me. Everything's going to be fine."

"Promise?"

"You bet!" But her smile faded when she walked back to Taffy. So far, nothing was fine.

Andi mounted with a heavy heart. She had utterly failed in her responsibility. She was stuck with a new, mean Troy and three scared little kids, and she had no idea where they were headed.

She brought Taffy alongside Betsy. "I'm ready."

Troy shook his head. "You're not coming."

"Oh yes, I am. I promised Justin I'd—"

"No." Troy cut her off. "You're going home to deliver a message. If I overheard Levi right when he was waving that letter around, Kate should be back tomorrow. Tell her to meet me in Denver, one week from today. She knows where. I'll have the children with me."

"Justin put me in charge of the kids. I can't leave them."

"You do what I say, or I'll take your horse and leave you out here."

"Then you'll hang as a horse thief!"

For a moment, Troy looked like he wanted to smack her. Then he cracked a smile, which quickly gave way to a low chuckle. "You Carters got more than your fair share of stubbornness, but it's not going to help you today."

Andi glared at her brother-in-law, daring him to make her leave.

Troy glanced at the sky. "It's starting to cloud up again. Looks like a storm's moving in." He lost his smile. "What's it going to be, Andi? A long, miserable walk home or a chance to ride? I don't care which you choose."

Andi slumped. She was outmatched. Troy was bigger than she was. If he pulled her off Taffy and rode away with her mare, she would be stranded. At all costs, she must keep her horse. She tightened her grip on the reins and nodded.

Troy grinned. "I'm glad to learn you have some sense, after all."

Andi ignored him. She looked at her nephew. "Good-bye, Levi. Look after Betsy and Hannah."

Levi rubbed his sleeve across his face and said nothing.

Betsy started crying.

"Nandi!" Hannah wailed. "Don't go!" She reached out her arms toward Andi, but Troy shoved them down. "Nandi! Mama!" She kicked and howled.

Troy held her in a tight grip. "That's enough, Hannah!"

Hannah kept shrieking.

Andi's heart turned over. If Hannah didn't stop crying, Troy would most likely smack her, or maybe even shake her.

What can I do to quiet her down? It was no use just talking to Hannah. Words were empty promises, especially to a hysterical three-year-old. What would calm her?

A quiet thought whispered inside Andi's head. *The locket.*

Her hand flew to her neck. *I can't. What would Justin say?*

He would say a child is more important than a trinket, even a costly one, the thought came back.

Before Andi changed her mind, she turned Taffy around and came alongside Troy. "Be quiet, Hannah. I have something special for you."

Hannah stopped crying. Her whole body shuddered.

Andi drew the precious locket from around her neck and held it out. "I can't go with you, Hannah, but here. This is for you and Tessie."

Hannah's face lit up. She curled her small fingers around the heart-shaped locket. "Lecklace," she said softly. "*My* lecklace?" She looked at Andi hopefully.

"For now." Andi blinked back tears. "I want you and Tessie to take care of my locket and keep it safe until I see you again. But you can only have it if you stop crying. Promise?"

Hannah nodded and smiled through her tears. "Tessie 'n me'll take care of it."

Andi's heart squeezed with love for the little girl. Hannah was no longer the irritating pest Andi had once considered her, but an adorable child with golden curls and a dimple in each cheek. Her round, blue eyes showed her wonder at Andi's gift.

"My lecklace," Hannah whispered. "Tessie's lecklace." She pulled her doll from under her arm and placed the chain around her neck. Then she leaned against her father's chest, popped her thumb in her mouth, and was silent.

Troy looked from Hannah to Andi and let out a sigh of relief. "That's better."

"I did it for Hannah," Andi said, "not for you."

"Well, whatever your reason, at least you shut her up." He tipped his hat in farewell, gave Coco's lead line a jerk, and headed out.

Andi sat helplessly on Taffy and watched Troy and the children disappear into the oak forest. A stiff breeze whipped across her face, and she shivered. She already missed her warm jacket. If she didn't start for home soon, she was going to get mighty cold.

She shook herself free of such thoughts. "I can't go home. Not without the kids. I could never face Kate . . . or Justin."

Hope surged unexpectedly. How long had they been gone? Perhaps Justin had sent Chad and the ranch hands after them by now. If she waited, she would have an entire ranch posse ready to go after Troy.

Andi's fingers shook as she drew out her brother's pocket watch. She popped it open and groaned. Just a little over an hour and a half had passed. She wouldn't even be missed for another half hour.

"I can't go home, and I can't wait around for help," she told Taffy. "I've got to go after them before I lose their trail. Are you going to help me?"

Taffy tossed her head and snorted, clearly ready to do anything but stand around in an empty field the rest of the afternoon.

Andi wished she hadn't been in such a hurry to give away her jacket. She stuffed the watch back in her pocket and sighed. "Well then, girl, I guess we'd better get going."

Chapter Fifteen

THE STORM

Andi had made the right decision—the only decision—about tracking Troy and the children, but uneasy prickles skittered up her neck just thinking about it. Troy would be furious when he discovered that instead of going home, Andi had followed him. How would he react?

She had other worries, as well. Even if she did manage to find the kids, how would she get them away from their father?

And then there was this miserable weather!

She glanced at the sky. Storm clouds were rolling in, piling up against the mountains in great heaps. Soon it would rain, washing out any tracks the horses might have left. "God," she prayed, "please keep the rain away until I figure out where they've gone."

Andi nudged Taffy into a trot and wound her way through the oaks, where she had last seen the group traveling. Tracks were easy to find. The ground was soft from the recent rains, and three horses' hooves chewed up the mixture of grass and dirt fairly well.

At first, it looked like Troy had circled back to follow the creek. Further on, the tracks took off cross-country, heading northwest. The trail wound its way into a gully between two hills, then up again and north for a mile or so.

Where in the world was Troy taking the children? There was nothing up here but lonely rangeland and a line shack or two.

"M-maybe he's going to spend the night in a l-line shack," Andi stammered between chattering teeth. It wasn't a bad choice. The line shacks were kept stocked and ready for any tired cowhand working far from the home ranch.

Andi hoped there was one close by. Even if Troy blew up at seeing her, surely he would let her stay. Her stomach was rumbling like thunder, and the afternoon light was beginning to fade. Great, black clouds raced overhead, threatening rain. A few drops fell against her cheeks. She brushed them aside and kept going.

The sound of running water a few minutes later brought Andi to a halt. She pulled back on Taffy's reins and slid from the saddle. Kneeling beside a small creek, she saw the faint tracks of at least one horse that had crossed.

She stood up and pondered. This had to be the creek that ran close to the northern boundary of the ranch. But what was north of the ranch?

"The river." The San Joaquin River, flowing south and west out of the mountains, was only a few miles away.

"Wait a minute." Andi snapped her fingers and mounted Taffy. "That abandoned t-town is up here somewhere, right n-next to the river. Troy would remember Millerton."

Talking to Taffy always helped her think things through. "There's got to be a few empty buildings left." She was certain Troy would find an old cabin—one that had been spared from past flooding—and spend the night. The next day, he would—

"What'll he do?" Andi asked Taffy as she urged the palomino across the creek. "Where will he go next?"

She chewed on her lip, trying to solve the puzzle. Denver was a long way from the Sierra foothills. How would he get back into the valley to catch the train? He certainly wouldn't chance backtracking to Fresno.

The gurgling creek gave Andi the answer. "That's it, Taffy! All he has to do is cross the San Joaquin. From there, it's less than twenty miles to Madera, over easy ground."

Her heart beat fast at the revelation. Surely Troy wouldn't try to cross the river with three young children! The rain was filling the streams and rivers to their banks.

More than ever, Andi was desperate to find Levi and the girls. But could she locate Millerton in the dwindling light—especially over rough country?

Several more raindrops splattered her face. Andi shivered and lowered her head against the chilly breeze. She was starting to ache clear to her bones. Thoughts of Nila's tamales wouldn't leave her head. And roast beef sandwiches. And pumpkin pie.

"Hey!" Taffy's gait had changed. They were no longer struggling up yet another hill filled with scratchy brush and an occasional oak or lonely pine. Taffy was trotting along on a level track.

Andi looked down. Beneath her lay an old road. It was overgrown with dead grass and brush, but she could see the faint outline of wheel ruts. She looked up. The road led northwest, straight toward the old town site.

"You f-found it, Taffy!"

Andi knew where she was now. She and Cory had ridden along this very road—though never this far north—many times during their explorations around the ranch. When she'd asked Chad what in the world a road was doing in the middle of nowhere, he explained it was once part of an old stage line that hugged the Sierra foothills for miles.

Andi guessed Troy knew as well as she did the path this road took through the ranch. "He's pr-probably used it quite a b-bit these past few weeks," she muttered with a stab of annoyance. "I b-bet Troy's holed up in a cabin around here, snug as you please, in front of a warm fire."

Andi clenched her teeth to stop them from chattering. "I wish I was holed up in front of a warm fire." She nudged Taffy into a slow, loping gait and gave the mare her head. Taffy was sure-footed. She wouldn't leave the road. The mare would bring Andi safely to the river and the abandoned town.

Andi was so pleased to be on the right track that she paid little attention when the small smattering of raindrops changed to a steady downpour. Then the clouds burst open and rain spilled out in great bucketfuls.

Within moments, Andi was drenched. A gust of wind drove the rain into her face. "Come on, girl," she urged Taffy. "Let's f-find a place to get out of this s-storm."

Without warning, a flash of lightning lit up the sky, followed by an earsplitting crack of thunder.

Taffy bolted.

Andi lost the reins and nearly flew from the saddle. With a cry of alarm, she clutched the saddle horn, hunkered down, and let Taffy run. She hadn't counted on a thunderstorm right over her head. Rain, yes. But this? Thunder and lightning were scary enough at home, when she could take refuge under her bedcovers, but here there was no place to hide.

She swallowed her terror and hung on.

Taffy gradually slowed to a nervous trot. Andi fumbled for the reins. Murmuring words she hoped would quiet her horse and calm her own racing heart, she sat up and brought Taffy to a halt. The mare still danced and tossed her head.

"Easy, girl." Andi swiped at the water running down her face. Why hadn't she worn a hat this afternoon? She peered through the twilight, hoping to find a place where she could get out of the rain. But she saw only dark clouds, gray rain, and the black outline of a few scraggly trees.

"Oh, T-taffy, I wish I'd never d-done this. I'm cold. I'm wet. And I'm s-scared. I'll never find them." She choked back a sob. "I won't cry. I won't!"

Another bolt of lightning flashed. Thunder crashed. Taffy reared.

Andi lost her grip. She fell from the saddle and landed on the ground with a *splat*. The next instant she was on her feet. She snatched at the dangling reins. "Stand still, Taffy."

Taffy refused to stand still. She shied away, threw her head back, and tried to break free from Andi's tight hold. The mare clearly wanted out of this storm, and *right now*!

"Whoa, girl." Andi soothed her friend. "I'm right here. I'm sorry I startled you by falling off." Her thoughts were screaming, but she forced herself to stay calm. She stroked Taffy's neck and kept talking. "I hate thunderstorms, and I can see that you do too. We'll never do *this* again, I promise."

Taffy whinnied.

"Another thing. When we get home, you've got to keep quiet about what just happened. I'll never hear the end of it if anybody finds out you dumped me."

Taffy began to settle down at the soothing words. She snorted, tossed her head, and then stood still.

"Good girl." Andi rubbed her horse's quivering flank. "Take it easy. We'll find shelter in no time. Be patient." She reached for the stirrup just as another flash of lightning tore open the sky.

Taffy lurched to one side, tearing the slippery reins from Andi's hands. Her head smacked into Andi, sending her to the ground. Free at last, the mare bolted into the night.

"No, Taffy! Come back!"

It was no use. For the first time in Andi's memory, her beloved horse was running away. Reins flapped around her neck. Stirrups bounced against her sides. Still she ran. Taffy clearly had no intention of stopping until she reached her warm, dry stable.

Andi sat in the middle of the old stage road and started to cry. Her horse was gone. She was all alone and chilled to the bone. The wind drove the rain through her clothing like it was made of tissue paper. What now?

"Please, God," she sobbed, "I've got to find shelter soon. I don't think I can make it out here in the storm much longer. I'm so cold and—"

Before she finished her desperate prayer, a faint flicker of yellow caught her gaze. She rubbed her eyes and squinted toward the pale, twinkling light. Off the road to her left, almost hidden in a cluster of oak and scrub pine, what looked like a cabin sat nestled on a small rise. When she looked again, the flicker became a small square. A window?

When another flash of lightning lit up the sky, Andi spied the dark outline of a cabin not more than twenty yards away. Her heart leaped. Ignoring the thunder, she jumped to her feet and raced up the incline. She sloshed her way through the rivulets pouring past her and soon found herself less than a dozen feet from her goal.

Caution brought her to a stop. What would Troy say when he saw her? Worse, what if this wasn't Troy's place? It might be a hermit's cabin, someone who didn't care for visitors.

Chills raced up Andi's spine. Years ago she and Cory had met a hermit. He was called Loony Lou for a reason. This was not his cabin, but what if—

The storm decided for her. Lightning and thunder ripped the air, and Andi threw caution to the wind. She dashed up to the door of the crude little cabin, lifted the latch, and burst through the opening.

The warmth of the tiny place engulfed her. She crumpled to the floor in a soggy heap and lay still. Letting out a grateful sigh, she closed her eyes and didn't care what happened to her next, so long as she was out of the storm.

Chapter Sixteen

A CHILLY WELCOME

Clamoring voices and tugging hands roused Andi from her dazed state. She opened her eyes. Levi knelt beside her on the floor, plucking at her sleeve. When he caught her eye, he shook his head. "Boy, that was dumb." But he looked overjoyed to see her.

Troy pushed past the children and yanked Andi to her feet. "Of all the outrageous, reckless stunts!" He gave her a shake. "I told you to go home."

Andi's teeth chattered so hard she couldn't speak. Fresh tears welled up. She didn't bother to wipe them away.

Troy shoved her aside. He stomped across the room, muttering under his breath. "Fool kid, tryin' to get herself killed."

Andi's legs just wouldn't hold her up and she collapsed again. Troy looked angry. Scary angry. Perhaps this hadn't been such a good idea after all. What if he decided to throw her out of the cabin and lock the door? *Please, no.* She couldn't go back out in that storm.

She curled up in a tight ball and stared at the fire. Small arms encircled her neck. "I'm glad you're here," Betsy whispered in her ear.

"Let her go, Betsy." Troy's hand clamped around Andi's arm. He pulled her up and half-dragged, half-carried her away from the fire.

Andi panicked. Was Troy throwing her outside? She twisted to free herself. "No, no! L-leave m-me alone. Let me go."

"Stop fussing. I'm not tossing you out, though I'm mighty tempted." Now across the room, Troy kicked a door open and thrust Andi through a dark opening. A bundle of clothes sailed in after her. "Change your clothes and get back to the fire, before you freeze to death." He turned on his heel and left, slamming the door so hard the cabin shook.

Andi gulped back a sob of fear and relief. *He's letting me stay. I can stay.* At least for now.

The lean-to was bitterly cold. The only light shone through narrow cracks in the inside wall. With trembling fingers, Andi unbuttoned her shirt and wrenched away the sopping fabric. It dropped to the floor with a loud *splat.* Shivering, she drew on a flannel shirt two sizes too big.

She pulled off her drenched riding skirt next, then her boots. Slipping on the britches Troy had given her, she rolled the cuffs above her ankles and straightened up.

Andi could not stop shaking. She clutched the waistband of the huge pair of pants and looked around the dim room. Spying a short length of rope lying in the corner, she snatched it up and threaded it through the belt loops on the pants. She gathered up her boots and wet clothes and made her way back to the main cabin.

Betsy ran to greet her. "Why is your face that funny color?"

"B-because I'm c-cold," Andi replied. She dropped her wet clothes in a corner and fumbled with the rope belt. Her fingers felt clumsy.

"Let me help," Levi said. He knotted the rope securely around her waist.

Betsy handed her a coarse woolen blanket. Andi drew it around her shoulders and huddled on the floor in front of the fire.

"Look!" Betsy giggled a few minutes later. "There's steam coming from your head. Are you cooking?"

"Leave her be," Troy snapped. He plopped down on the bed and glared at her from across the room. "Where's your horse?"

Andi clutched the blanket tighter around her shoulders. Warmth from the fire slowly began to inch its way into her body. "She got scared in the storm and threw me. Then she ran off."

Troy slammed his fist against the wall. "That horse will head straight for home. Before morning, every cowhand on your ranch will be scouring the hills for you." He rose from the bed and began pacing.

"They're looking for us already." Andi didn't need Justin's pocket watch to tell her they were long overdue. "We should have been back hours ago. Chad's probably steaming mad right now."

At least it wasn't Andi's fault this time.

Troy crossed the room and grasped Andi's shoulders. "Why couldn't you do what you were told?" He gave her a shake.

Hannah began to cry.

Andi jerked out of Troy's grasp and glared up at him. "Come here, Hannah." She opened her arms to the little girl. Hannah ran to Andi and threw her arms around her.

Andi looked past Hannah's golden head and into Troy's eyes. "Justin said the children were my responsibility. I can't go home without them."

"That's what *you* think, my stubborn little sister-in-law." Troy planted his hands on his hips. "Just because I let you dry off in my cabin doesn't mean I'm going to change my mind. At first light, the kids and I are heading out. Without a horse, you'll be forced to either walk home or stay here. Either way, you won't be following us."

"You're going to Madera," Andi said, "to catch the train."

"How—" Troy's face showed his astonishment. He let out a breath. "Think you're pretty smart, don't you? Well, so what? By the time anyone finds you, we'll be clean out of the state. Don't forget to give Katie my message."

"But the river! It's got to be high, especially after this storm. It's dangerous. Hannah's so little."

"Shut up!" Troy grabbed a bottle of whiskey and threw himself on the bed. "Another word, and I'll toss you out of here, storm or no storm."

He took a swig of the liquid, corked the bottle, and stashed it under the mattress. "Now, I've had quite a day, so I'm hitting the sack." He pulled a hat from a nail overhead and covered his face. "Keep everybody quiet, m'girl, or I'll take a strap to you." He clasped his hands behind his head, let out a long sigh, and relaxed.

Before long, he was snoring.

Andi woke with a start. She lifted her head from the table. Although she was as warm as she could hope with bare feet and wet hair, she was weary beyond belief. Struggling through the storm had worn her out.

"Aren't you hungry?" Levi set a plate of cold beans and hardtack down in front of her.

Andi couldn't muster the energy to answer. She picked up the fork and forced herself to take a few bites. *This is worse than beef jerky*, she mused.

She turned her attention to Betsy and Hannah. The girls lay curled in front of the fire on an old blanket. Another blanket covered them. They looked warm and cozy.

Andi envied them. She wanted to close her eyes and sleep away the worries and chills and body aches. She wished she could fall asleep and wake up to find out this afternoon and evening had been only a horrible dream.

But wishing would not get her out of this fix. Wishing would not return the children to Kate. No, it was up to Andi. She had a job to do, and she was going to do it. While Troy slept, she would gather the children and leave. She would take them back to Katherine if it was the last thing she ever did.

Earlier, she had whispered her plan to Levi. He looked scared but agreed to go along with it. "Justin said I'm supposed to mind you, remember? You tell me what to do, and I'll do it."

Andi knew that behind Levi's brave words, he wanted his mother as much as Betsy and Hannah did.

They had put the little girls to bed and stayed awake to make plans, until Andi fell asleep over the table. She needed rest, and they couldn't leave until Troy was sleeping soundly.

"Is it time to go yet?" Levi asked when Andi shoved the plate of cold food away. He glanced at Troy, who hadn't moved a muscle. "It's way past midnight."

"Has the storm passed?" Without a sound, Andi rose from the bench and approached the one tiny window. She cupped her hands to either side of her face and strained to see through the blackness. "The clouds seem to be breaking up. Perhaps there's a moon hidden somewhere behind them."

Levi came and stood beside her. "We're gonna take the horses, aren't we?"

Andi nodded. She didn't want to take them. They had a better chance of sneaking away and staying hidden without the added bother of getting the horses ready. But it was either take the horses or carry Hannah . . . maybe even Betsy. She couldn't pack around a sleeping child. Neither could Levi.

Besides, Andi didn't want Troy to be able to follow them when he awoke and found them gone. "I'll get the horses ready. You stay inside."

Levi handed Andi her jacket. She drew it on over the flannel shirt and crossed the room to retrieve her boots. They were still damp inside, and cold. She made a face when she pulled them on. In spite of her fear of staying, she really, *really* hated to leave this cozy cabin.

Andi cracked the door. It slid open with only the whisper of a creak. Taking a deep breath, she slipped through the narrow opening and into the chilly night air.

Once outside, all the terror of earlier that evening rushed over

Andi like a flood. She pushed it aside and looked up. The clouds raced across the sky, revealing a few bright stars and a pale half-moon. It wasn't much light, but it lit the crude shed where the horses were stabled. She ducked around the three-sided building and peeked inside.

The horses were tied securely to a feed box. Troy's large gelding danced and pulled at his rope. Andi could see the whites of his eyes in the pale light. She would have a difficult time keeping this huge animal under control in his present state. It would be madness to take him along.

She called to Patches and Coco. The two smaller animals nickered unhappy greetings. And no wonder. Troy had not bothered to unsaddle any of the horses.

"I'm sorry, fellas. He's sure no horseman." Andi rubbed their noses. "But he's saved me a bit of work." She spoke gently while she untied them and led them out of the shelter.

The moment she left the lean-too, a loud, insistent whinny pierced the air. She caught her breath and hurried back to the remaining horse. He appeared frantic to be let loose.

Well, why not? They couldn't ride him, and they couldn't leave him to alert Troy with his screams. *Why not cut him loose and let him run?*

Putting her thoughts into action, Andi cut the horse free from his halter. With a snort and a whinny, he whirled around and sped off into the night. "Good riddance, and don't you dare come back," she whispered.

After tying Patches and Coco to a tree a safe distance away, she returned to the cabin. Creeping inside, she found a white-faced Levi staring at her.

"What's going on? Pa jerked in his sleep when he heard the horse scream."

Andi shot a panicked look in Troy's direction. He lay sprawled across the bed on his stomach, one arm dangling over the edge.

Thankfully, he looked sound asleep. "Your pa's horse didn't like being alone. I let him go."

"Let him go? Why?"

"He's in no state to be ridden. He's too spooked."

Levi accepted Andi's judgment with a loud sigh. Then he followed her to where Hannah and Betsy lay sleeping. They had dressed the girls in their coats and shoes before settling them for the night. All they had to do was pick them up and carry them to the horses.

"You get Hannah," Andi said. "I'll wake Betsy."

Levi reached down. Blanket and all, he scooped his sister and her doll up in his arms. He staggered backward a few steps before catching his balance. Hannah didn't stir. Neither did Troy.

Andi opened the cabin door for the pair and turned back to Betsy. The little girl was too heavy to carry, so she bent down, covered the child's mouth with her hand, and whispered in her ear, "Come on, Betsy. It's time to go home."

Betsy's usual response to the unexpected was a high-pitched shriek. Andi had heard it more than once during the past month, and she dreaded it now. Sure enough, Betsy sat up with a start and filled her lungs with air.

Andi kept her hand over Betsy's open mouth. "Hush."

Betsy's eyes were wide with fear and glassy from sleep, but for once she obeyed Andi and kept quiet. Andi snatched up the blankets, took Betsy's hand, and led her out into the night.

Once outside, Betsy began to whimper. "I'm cold. I'm tired."

"Shh. I'll help you in a minute." Andi took Hannah from Levi so he could mount Coco. As soon as he was settled, she passed the sleeping child to him. "Whatever you do, don't drop Hannah's doll."

Levi stuffed Tessie under the blanket before wrapping his arms around Hannah. He looked frightened but determined. Hannah moaned, but then she found her thumb and was quiet.

"How am I supposed to hold onto Hannah and stay on this pony at the same time?" Levi whispered in a shaky voice. "She's limp as a rag."

"Use your stirrups. Grab the saddle horn when you feel unsteady. I'll take the lead rope in a minute." She swung into the saddle on Patches's back. Betsy reached out her arms. It took all of Andi's strength to pull her niece and the blanket up on the horse.

Betsy let out a sleepy sigh.

Andi tucked the blanket around Betsy and nudged the paint horse. "Come on, Patches, let's go home." She took the lead rope from Levi's outstretched hand and turned Patches toward the old stage road.

They were on their way.

Chapter Seventeen

INTO THE NIGHT

I'm tired." Levi shifted the sleeping Hannah to a different position. "Hannah's slipping all over the place no matter how tight I hold her—"

Coco whinnied. One of his front legs buckled. The pony went down, sending Levi and Hannah over his head and onto the ground.

"Andi!" Levi yelped.

Hannah woke up with a shriek. "Mama!"

"This was a stupid, stupid idea!" Levi shouted up at Andi. He pushed the crying Hannah aside and jumped to his feet.

Hannah bawled louder.

"We're lost," Levi yelled. "I know we're lost. We've been riding around in circles for hours. I haven't seen or heard that creek you were talking about. It's starting to rain again, and I'm cold. I want to go back to the cabin."

Andi could barely see Levi, even though he stood only a few feet away. The night had closed in around them when the clouds rolled back in and covered the moon. With the pale light now hidden, the four children were plunged into darkness.

They had followed the old stage road for as long as Andi dared. Sooner or later they would have to leave it and set out over uneven, rolling rangeland in order to get back to the ranch. The terrain was littered with brush, trees, rocks, and gullies—a dangerous route to travel in the dark.

But it was the only route Andi knew to get back to the creek. She'd hoped to find it soon after they left the road. Although it would take longer, they could follow the creek out of the hills and into the valley. Once on level ground, Andi could easily find her way home.

That was her plan, anyway. It was so simple. So direct. So sensible. "So why isn't it working?" she grumbled.

Andi had led them over the rough country, stopping every so often to listen for the sound of running water. After an hour, she still hadn't heard the familiar rushing of her favorite creek. She'd even given Patches his head, hoping he'd lead them home. If he was, she decided wearily, he was certainly taking the long way around.

Hannah continued to sob. Andi shook Betsy. "Wake up. I have to take care of Hannah."

Betsy woke up with a cry. She clutched Patches's mane. "Are we home yet?"

"No." Andi dismounted and pulled Betsy from the saddle. "Come with me." She took her hand and followed the sound of wailing.

Andi nearly tripped over Hannah in the dark. She fell to the ground, gathered the little girl into her arms, and leaned back against a large boulder. She pulled the blanket around Hannah, drawing her close.

Levi shuffled over. He sat down beside Andi, rubbing his eyes and yawning. "We're never going to find our way back. The rain will wash us away and nobody'll ever find us. Nobody."

At Levi's gloomy words, Betsy set up a wail. She shoved her way onto Andi's lap. "Don't let the rain wash me away," she pleaded.

Andi winced when Betsy's full weight smashed down on her legs. *What can I do? In a few minutes, I'll be crying too. Are we really lost?*

In her heart, Andi knew Levi was right. They were lost. Perhaps in daylight she could find her way home, but it was useless to tramp around in total darkness. She was so tired she'd soon be falling asleep on horseback.

"The rain won't wash us away, Betsy," Andi mumbled. "It's hardly coming down."

She leaned her head back against the rock and let the raindrops splash her face. Closing her eyes, she sent up a desperate prayer. *Lord, I know I'm in charge, but I don't know what to do. Please show me how to get out of this fix so nobody gets hurt. Show me the way home!*

Before she could finish her prayer, Andi found herself drifting off to sleep.

Levi's shaking roused her. "Don't go to sleep, Andi."

Is that the answer? Sleep and wait for the daylight? Andi blinked. "I don't think we can go any farther tonight. We have to find someplace to rest."

"I'm for that," Levi said. He pointed into the darkness. "Is that a tree? Maybe we can crawl under it and get out of the rain."

Andi nodded. She and Levi gathered up the two little girls and their blankets, and staggered to the dark outline of a crooked old digger pine. It wasn't much shelter, but they crawled gratefully beneath the branches and curled up together for warmth.

Within minutes, they were fast asleep.

Andi opened her eyes to a damp and dreary morning. Although the rain had stopped, water continued to drip steadily from the overhead branches. She wiped the moisture from her face and groaned.

I feel terrible. Every muscle of Andi's body ached. Worse, her throat hurt and her nose felt stuffy. *What do you expect from spending a night under a tree in the rain?*

Inches away, the two little girls lay wrapped up in the blankets, fast asleep. Only the top of Hannah's head showed. Andi peeked under the blanket and found Hannah curled up like a round, silky kitten. Next to her, curled up just as tight, Betsy was breathing softly.

The girls appeared none the worse for their all-night adventure. They looked warm and dry. Andi wrapped her arms around herself and shivered. She felt cold and wet. Her feet, especially, were chunks of ice in her clammy boots.

She looked over at Levi. He was still asleep, his arm flung across his sisters' blanket. He sniffled in his sleep, then rolled over and coughed. With a start, he sat up.

"Where are we?" he croaked, wiping the sleep from his eyes.

"Under that tree you found last night. I think it kept most of the rain off." Andi sneezed. "I feel terrible. Let's get the horses and go home. I'm sure I can find my way in the daylight."

"Good." Levi nodded. "I don't feel so good myself." He coughed again. "And I'm hungry."

Andi crawled out from under the digger pine and stood up. She looked around. A sinking feeling entered her hollow stomach. "I don't see the horses." She swallowed. Her throat stung. "I don't remember tying them up. Did you?"

"Me?" Levi's eyes grew huge. "No. I didn't think about it. I was too tired. Didn't you?"

Andi shook her head. "I don't remember much about last night, except leaving the cabin." She stumbled a few yards and scanned the horizon. "They're nowhere."

Levi joined her. "At least we got this." He reached down and picked up Hannah's doll. Tessie was soaking wet. "She's still got that locket around her neck."

Andi sucked in her breath. *Thank you, God!* She longed to take the locket back, but she thought better of it. Hannah would notice a missing locket right away and start howling.

Levi handed Tessie to Andi. "What are we going to do?"

"Do?" Andi raised her eyebrows. "We're going to walk."

Levi looked over at his sleeping sisters. "Them too?"

"Unless you're going to carry them." Andi sneezed. "We might come across the horses later." She pointed toward a low rise in the distance. "I think the creek's that way."

Levi followed her gaze, turning a full circle. "Except for those tall mountains over there, everything looks alike. How can you tell one hill from another?"

She couldn't. The only landmark she recognized was the Sierra Nevada range, whose peaks were hidden under a veil of low, gray clouds. She knew, though, that the creek had to be somewhere in the direction she was pointing.

"Come on. The sooner we get started, the sooner we'll get home."

They roused the girls, who responded with whining and complaints. Andi thrust Tessie into Hannah's hands to quiet her. "Come on, sweetie. Let's go."

When Betsy learned the horses were gone, she howled. "I'm too tired to walk."

"You can stay here then," Levi told her.

Betsy shut her mouth and jumped up. Hannah clutched Tessie. She stuck her thumb in her mouth and took Andi's hand.

"We'll walk awhile, then rest. Then maybe I'll give you a piggyback ride." Andi picked up a blanket, draped it around her own shoulders, and squeezed Hannah's hand.

Levi picked up the other blanket and ran to catch up. "When do you think we'll get home?" A cough racked his body. "It's seven o'clock right now."

Andi whirled. "How on earth do you know—"

"I got a watch." Levi held up Justin's watch.

"Give that to me." She let go of Hannah and swiped for the pocket watch.

Levi was too quick. He dodged Andi. "If it wasn't for me, Uncle Justin's watch would still be back at the cabin in your riding skirt." He stuffed it in his pocket.

Andi deflated. Levi was right. Besides, she felt too lousy to wrestle him for it. "Fine, but you'd best take care of it."

"Better than *you!*" He laughed.

Andi shook her head. "Watch or no watch, it's going to take a long time to get home. Maybe all day, unless we find the horses."

Levi groaned.

"Taffy's home by now," she added when she saw Levi's hopeless expression. "I'm sure everyone's looking for us. They'll find us in no time."

Levi smiled weakly. "You think so?"

"Sure!" She didn't add how big the ranch really was and how it might take hours or even days to find four children wandering around the vast rangeland. She knew their only hope of discovery lay in following the creek.

The little group trudged on. They slipped and slid down brushy slopes into gullies, where water still ran from the storm the night before. Sloshing through the water, they made their way up the other side. Andi decided that the Circle C didn't look nearly as pretty on foot as it did from the back of a fast horse.

Walking became easier when the ground leveled off. Andi hoisted Hannah to her back. "Hang on."

"Giddy up!" Hannah squealed. She clutched Andi around the neck and bounced up and down on her back. "Faster, horsey!"

Andi winced. "I can't go any faster, Hannah. I'm a sick, tired old mare. I want to find my stable and take a nap."

Hannah giggled. "Funny Nandi." She balanced her doll on the top of Andi's head. "Look, Betsy. Tessie's riding too."

Andi gave Hannah a ride for a few minutes. When she could carry her no longer, she sank to her knees and set her down. "That's enough, Hannah. This horse has got to rest."

She swallowed painfully and rubbed her itchy nose. Tears welled up. *I want Mother. Or Justin. Or even Chad.*

She didn't think she could keep going. Levi was coughing longer

131

and more often. He looked exhausted. Hannah laid her head in Andi's lap.

Betsy leaned against Andi's shoulder. "I wish I had a cup of hot chocolate," she said wistfully.

"Hush!" Levi commanded.

Andi rushed to Betsy's defense. "You don't have to talk so mean to her."

"Shh!" Levi stood up. "I think I hear the creek."

Andi pushed the girls aside and leaped to her feet. She listened. "You're right. I hear it too. Come on." With renewed energy, she grabbed Hannah's hand and took off toward the sound of running water.

A few minutes later, they stood on the bank of the swollen creek. Andi grinned. "I know exactly where we are. We're upstream, about a mile from my favorite spot. All we have to do is follow the creek to my spot, then head for home. I know the way from there."

She turned to Levi. "It's still a long walk, but at least it's easy going. And it's downhill."

"Look!" Betsy squealed and pointed. "A horse. Maybe we can ride."

Andi spun around in joy. At last! Someone from the ranch had spotted them. Then her smile faded. She clenched her fists in alarm. "Oh no," she whispered. "It's Troy. His horse must have gone back to the cabin. I'm pretty sure he's tracking us!"

Chapter Eighteen

NO PLACE TO RUN

Andi dove behind a clump of scraggly willows and pulled the girls down with her.

Levi fell to her side, breathing hard. "What are we going to do?" He shook in fear.

"We're going to hide," Andi shot back. "I'm not letting Troy have you, not after all we've been through."

"He's coming too quick," Levi said. "He'll find us and . . . and oh, Andi! He's gonna be mad as a peeled rattler for what you did." Tears sprang to his eyes. He threw his arms around her. "I won't let Pa hurt you. I'll kick him if I have to."

Andi returned Levi's hug, and then untangled his arms. "Don't worry about me. We'll hide real good." She lifted Hannah over a clump of scratchy bushes and motioned to Levi and Betsy. "Get down here, as close to the creek as you can."

"These bushes don't make for much cover," Levi worried aloud.

"It's the best we've got. Now hush!"

They huddled just above the edge of the creek. Andi could feel it lapping at her heels. She hoped they wouldn't fall in. As swollen as the creek was, it could pull them away in a moment's time.

She wrapped her arms around Hannah and held her close. "Nobody make a sound."

For what seemed like hours, they lay motionless. But Andi knew

133

only a few minutes had passed when she peeked through the winter-dead brush. Her breath caught. Troy's horse was trotting along the creek, but some distance away.

She thanked God for the brush. It made it impossible for Troy to bring his horse closer to the creek at this spot. The undergrowth covered both banks for nearly a hundred yards up and downstream.

As long as we stay quiet, maybe he'll pass right by us, Andi thought.

Troy would have to dismount if he wanted to search closer to the stream. Once he left his horse, Andi would have a chance to snatch it. She'd gallop right over the top of him if she had to. Anything to escape.

The plan made her smile.

Troy's voice startled her. "I know you kids are here. I saw you from the top of the rise. Why don't you make it easy on yourselves and come out?"

Hannah whimpered. Levi clapped his hand over her mouth. "If you so much as peep," he hissed in her ear, "I'll toss Tessie in the creek."

Hannah's eyes grew round at the threat. She swallowed her sob and clutched Tessie to her chest. She scowled at her brother, but she didn't make another sound.

The four children lay next to the creek, flat on their stomachs. Dead branches poked them in their sides. Brambles caught in their hair. Water splashed over their feet. Andi couldn't think of a more wretched hiding place.

She considered showing herself to Troy. He'd be angry, but he'd take Levi and the girls to a dry place. He would probably leave her here to fend for herself, but anything would be better than lying in the cold, squishy mud. Her throat was on fire. Her nose was stuffed up so much she couldn't take a decent breath. Her head ached.

I can't do it! She couldn't give the kids to Troy. She couldn't let Justin down. She would never be able to face Kate. Even God might be disappointed in her for thinking only of herself and how rotten she felt. She shook her head. No, she would not let Troy—

Ah-choo!

Levi stared at Andi in horror.

Andi rubbed her nose and willed the next sneeze to go away. It didn't work. As soon as she took her hand away, she sneezed again. *Oh no!*

Branches snapped, and suddenly Troy stood above them. "I've had it with you four." He reached down and yanked Hannah to him. "Get up out of this muck."

Hannah screamed.

"Let her go!" Andi launched herself at Troy's legs. He fell backward, crashing into the bushes. Hannah wriggled from his arms. "Run. Get the horse!" Andi shouted.

Levi, Betsy, and Hannah scrambled like frightened rabbits.

Troy shook Andi away as if she weighed no more than a pebble. He lurched to his feet, entangling himself in the underbrush.

Andi jumped up and grabbed Troy around the waist. She prayed for strength to hold him long enough for Levi and the girls to mount up and ride away.

"Hurry!" she screamed. "Ride far and fast!" She didn't care what Troy did to her, so long as the children got away.

Troy reached behind his back, grabbed Andi's arms, and jerked free. "You're nothing but a burr under my saddle."

Andi yelped and grabbed for his shirt. Troy gave her a shove that sent her stumbling backward. She landed in the soft mud next to the creek.

Furious at herself for not being able to hang on longer, she clambered up the embankment and tried to knock Troy to the ground.

"Don't you *ever* give up?" He grabbed her wrists and flung her away.

Andi did not land in the mud this time. She lost her balance, tripped over a low-lying bush, and fell backward. The shock of icy water tore a scream from her throat.

Terror slammed into Andi's mind as quickly as the swirling water closed in around her body. This creek was not the worn-out, muddy trickle from a month ago. It was a wild, raging flood. It slashed at her arms and legs when she tried to stand up. Her feet were swept downstream. A branch struck her face.

Flailing her arms, Andi broke the surface and gulped a breath of air. In that brief second, she realized she was traveling fast—faster than anyone could run. If she didn't reach the creek bank soon, she'd be well on her way out of the foothills and into the valley.

There would be no rescue. Troy wanted her out of the way, and he'd managed that pretty well. Besides, she was so far downstream by now that he probably couldn't catch her even if he wanted to, and she was sure he didn't.

Andi found the strength to pull in one more breath of air. She was losing the battle. She couldn't see anything but the foaming, muddy water. She couldn't hear anything but the roar of the creek devouring her. *God, please—*

A searing, ripping pain suddenly shot through her head. She gasped. To her surprise, her lungs didn't fill with water. The pain continued. Something was yanking on her hair, pulling her from the water. A moment later, strong arms dragged her from the freezing current. She felt herself dumped on the cold, soggy creek bank.

Andi moaned and immediately threw up. She lay in the mud and gagged and choked, then threw up some more. Then she lay still. She was too weak to do anything else.

"Fool kid."

Andi forced her eyes open. Troy stood over her, gasping for breath and staring at her with dark, haunted eyes. He was soaked from head to foot. "You're nothing but trouble, Andrea Carter," he said between breaths. "If it weren't for you, I'd be miles away by now. I should have left you in the creek."

Andi lay on her side, confused and freezing. She shook so much she could barely speak. "B-but you d-didn't leave me. You s-saved me. Why?"

Troy lifted Andi into his arms. "I don't rightly know," he admitted with a frown. He settled her on his horse and climbed up behind her. "When I saw you tumble into the creek I just lit out as fast as I could to get ahead of you." He shivered. "I already regret it. That water's *cold*."

But Troy no longer sounded angry. Only tired, and maybe a bit frightened by what had happened. He nudged his horse into a trot. "Let's get back to the kids."

They rode in silence for a few minutes, with only the sound of the rushing water in their ears. Then Troy said, "You've ruined all my plans, you know."

Andi didn't reply. She was too cold to do anything but clamp her jaw shut to keep her teeth from chattering.

Troy slowed his horse to a walk near a grove of trees upstream, where Levi and his sisters crouched under an oak. Levi had his arms around Betsy and Hannah, holding them close. All three were sobbing.

"Quit your blubbering!" Troy reined his horse to a stop. "Here she is, wet and cold, but alive." He dismounted and lifted Andi from the horse. Then he carried her over to the children and set her down.

Levi wrapped both blankets around Andi's shoulders. "Please say you're gonna be fine, Andi. Please."

Andi nodded. She hoped it wasn't a lie. Right now, she felt far from fine.

Levi rubbed away his tears and faced his father. "Pa," he said in a trembling voice, "I'm not going with you. I'm staying with Andi 'til somebody comes for her. She's too cold and sick to leave out here by herself."

Troy said nothing.

"You can holler as loud as you like, or beat me, or try to drag me off, but it won't do no good. I'm not going. Neither are Betsy and Hannah. What you did to Andi ain't decent. I saw you push her in."

"I brought her back," Troy growled.

Levi scowled. "Kinfolk don't treat each other that way. If you want to be an outlaw, you go ahead. But do it by yourself." He snagged his father's hat from the ground and held it out. "Here's your hat. Now go away and leave us alone."

Shaking with cold, Andi tried to focus on Levi's bold words. If Troy decided to take his children, there was nothing Levi could do about it. He was too little to put up a fight.

There was nothing Andi could do about it either. She'd lost, but she was too numb to care. All she wanted was a warm bed, a hot drink, and her mother.

Troy didn't say anything. He didn't take the hat. He stood with his hands on his hips and stared at the bedraggled group huddled under the tree. Then he dropped his hands to his sides. His shoulders slumped, as if rescuing Andi from the creek had washed all of the fight out of him.

He took his hat and shoved it down on his head. "You've got yourself a mighty smart mouth, boy," he finally said. "But . . . I reckon you're right."

"Pa?"

"I got no choice but to leave you here." Troy didn't sound happy about it. "I saw how fast that creek carried Andi away. It's no good trying to take you kids across the San Joaquin." He shuddered. "I'd be a fool to try."

Levi gaped at his father.

"Chasing after you four all morning has cost me too much time, and I'm down to one horse. I'll be lucky to save my own skin now." Troy shook his head. "I don't plan to stick around until your uncles show up, so I'm leaving."

Troy mounted his big, black gelding. "So long. Tell your mother she hasn't seen the last of me." He looked at Andi. "When I told you

I didn't know how to repay you for pulling me out of the mud last month, you said I would do the same for you." He touched two fingers to the brim of his hat in a cocky salute. "Well, I reckon we're square now. Paid in full."

Andi nodded. She tried to speak, but no words could squeeze past her icy lips. Her thoughts, however, were spinning faster than a top. *He's leaving. He's leaving. Thank you, God! He's leaving the kids here.* Tears of gratitude welled up in her eyes.

Troy turned his horse and galloped back the way he'd come, toward old Millerton.

Andi watched until Troy and his horse were only a speck in the distance.

Chapter Nineteen

FAREWELL

Andi woke up coughing. It hurt like fire. And she was so cold. Although she lay under mountains of quilts, she shivered uncontrollably. *I feel terrible. Where's Mother?*

Andi didn't know how she'd come to be lying in her own bed, but she knew somebody must have found them after Troy rode off. She recalled Levi shaking her and yelling, "Wake up, Andi! They're here."

She remembered opening her eyes long enough to see Levi throwing himself into Mitch's arms, and the little girls jumping up and down. Her memory was a jumble of mixed-up images. Worried faces. Questions that made no sense. Trying to stay upright on a galloping horse.

Then nothing.

It didn't matter. It was enough to wake up and find herself home at last, home where she could get warm and dry. She'd soaked in a hot tub and gone to bed. How long ago had that been? And why did she still feel so lousy?

"Andi?" A voice gently called her from her fevered thoughts.

She opened her eyes. Katherine stood above her, smiling. She held a covered tray in her hands. "Do you feel like eating?"

Andi shook her head and coughed. It was harsh and deep.

Katherine's expression turned worried. "I want you to try a little of this soup. Nila made a huge pot of chicken broth for you and Levi."

"How's Levi?" she croaked.

"He's sick too, although he's recovering faster. You both came down with bad chest colds. Dr. Weaver was afraid yours might go into pneumonia."

"Where's Mother?"

"She'll be up directly. Right now she's resting."

Andi coughed again. "How long have I been sick?"

"Four days," Katherine replied. "But this is the first day you've been awake long enough to give me trouble. The rest of the week you drank your broth and took your medicine like a good girl."

"Four days!" She tried to sit up. "Are Betsy and Hannah all right?" Coughing, she fell back against her pillow.

"They're fine," Katherine assured her. "Runny noses and all."

"Justin's going to have a fit. He told me to take care of the kids." Hot tears trickled down Andi's cheeks. "I didn't do a very good job. I tried, Kate. I really did. I followed Troy and found the kids. We escaped, but when I fell in the creek I knew it was the end. I was too cold. I sat under a tree and didn't care what happened anymore."

Katherine set the tray aside and sat down on the bed. "You're wrong, Andi. Justin's proud of you. And I'm so grateful. We heard the whole story from Levi. Every last detail. You didn't give up. I've sat by your bedside these four days and thanked God for you and prayed that you would get well."

Andi relaxed. Justin was proud of her. The children were safe. She smiled.

Katherine picked up a small object that lay on the nightstand. "Here's your locket. Safe and sound." She lifted Andi's hand and laid it in her palm. "Hannah and Tessie took good care of it."

Andi curled her fingers around the precious necklace. "I bet Hannah screamed when you tried to take it."

"Why no, she didn't," Katherine said. "Not a peep. I gave her mine instead."

Andi wrinkled her forehead in confusion. "What?"

"Mother found my old locket, the one Father gave me for *my* tenth birthday." Katherine chuckled at Andi's expression. "You and Melinda aren't the only girls in this family to receive a special locket. Father started the tradition with me."

Her eyes grew misty. "I miss him."

"So do I," Andi said softly. For the first time, she sensed a connection with her sister that she hadn't experienced before. It felt . . . nice. "Help me with my locket, will you?"

Katherine strung the gold chain around Andi's neck.

"Do you know what happened to Troy?" Andi asked when Katherine sat back. "Has anyone tracked him down?"

Katherine shook her head. "It looks like he got clean away. The storm wiped out any chance of tracking him. Besides, our brothers had more on their minds that day than going after Troy. They wanted to get you, Levi, and the little girls home."

"Are you"—a tickle in her throat threw Andi into a coughing spell—"are you glad he got away?"

Katherine didn't answer. She reached for the chicken soup and a spoon.

"*I'm* glad," Andi blurted. "That sounds awful, doesn't it? But after he rescued me from the creek, Troy seemed different somehow, at least a little bit. He acted more like TJ Silver and less like Troy. Maybe he'll do some serious thinking about right and wrong, maybe even turn himself in."

"I don't know, Andi." She sounded sad.

"God sure straightened *me* up last spring," Andi told her. "He could do the same with Troy, if only Troy would give Him a chance. Don't you think?"

"I hope so, little sister. I really do." Katherine smiled. "Now, are you going to eat this soup like a good girl, or am I going to have to spoon-feed you?"

"Good-bye, Levi," Andi said two weeks later, standing with him at the Fresno train depot. She had already hugged and said good-bye to Betsy, Hannah, and even Tessie, who wore Katherine's special "lecklace" around her battered neck. "I wish you'd stay for Christmas. It's only a week away."

"Aw, Andi. Don't start that again," Levi said. "You know Mama promised Aunt Rebecca we'd spend our first Christmas with her in her fancy house in San Francisco." He shrugged. "I hear she's a lonely old lady, just waiting to spoil three little kids."

"Aunt Rebecca will spoil you, all right." *And hopefully she'll stop nagging Mother about me.* She threw her arms around her nephew. "I'll miss you. Come back next summer and you can be a ranch boy. We could work together. Chad says I'm finally getting old enough to be useful with a lasso."

Levi backed away and smoothed his new suit. "Don't start acting like a sissy girl. No mushy stuff." He crossed the platform. "When's the train coming, Mama? If it doesn't come soon, Andi's gonna talk me into staying and becoming a cowpoke."

Katherine laughed. "You'd make a good one, son. Your uncles have taught you a lot in the short time we've been here."

"You'll come back for a visit real soon, won't you, Kate?" Andi asked. "I'm going to miss you." She grinned. "I never thought I'd hear myself say *that*. I'm ashamed that I used to wish you hadn't come back."

Katherine drew Andi into a warm embrace. "It's all right. We all do things we regret and have to ask forgiveness for. You only have to look at my own life to see that. My biggest regret is that I didn't come home and make things right sooner."

The sound of a train whistle cut through the air.

"I guess this is good-bye," Katherine whispered to Andi. "I love you."

Andi backed away from her sister. "I love you too, Kate."

When the train pulled out of the station twenty minutes later, Andi stood with the rest of her family and waved good-bye to Katherine and the children. *It's not really good-bye*, Andi decided. *They won't be living that far away.*

She watched the train gather speed. The cars looked dark against the glowing winter sunset. *With Kate and the kids in San Francisco, maybe it wouldn't be so bad to visit Aunt Rebecca, after all.*

Then she grimaced. *What am I thinking?* But as she climbed into the carriage for the ride home, the words *well, maybe someday* kept time with the steady beat of the horses' hooves.

A literature unit study guide with enrichment activities is available for *Andrea Carter and the Family Secret* as a free download at CircleCAdventures.com.

Contact Susan K. Marlow at susankmarlow@kregel.com.